# ORANGE STORM

ORANGE STORM SERIES #1

NED MARCUS

ORANGE LOG PUBLISHING

Copyright © 2021 by Ned Marcus

1st edition (paperback)

ISBN 978-986-95833-8-1

All rights reserved.

No part of this book may be reproduced in any form or by any electronic or mechanical means, including information storage and retrieval systems, without written permission from the author, except for the use of brief quotations in a book review.

This book is a work of fiction. The characters, places and events are products of the author's imagination or have been used fictitiously and are not to be construed as real. Any resemblance to persons, living or dead, is entirely coincidental.

Published by Orange Log Publishing

Cover Design by Damonza

# CONTENTS

| | |
|---|---:|
| Chapter 1 | 1 |
| Chapter 2 | 6 |
| Chapter 3 | 13 |
| Chapter 4 | 25 |
| Chapter 5 | 32 |
| Chapter 6 | 36 |
| Chapter 7 | 43 |
| Chapter 8 | 52 |
| Chapter 9 | 58 |
| Chapter 10 | 68 |
| Chapter 11 | 75 |
| Chapter 12 | 80 |
| Chapter 13 | 87 |
| Chapter 14 | 95 |
| Chapter 15 | 104 |
| Chapter 16 | 114 |
| Chapter 17 | 124 |
| Chapter 18 | 136 |
| Chapter 19 | 145 |
| Chapter 20 | 156 |
| Chapter 21 | 163 |
| Chapter 22 | 169 |
| Chapter 23 | 177 |
| Chapter 24 | 185 |
| Chapter 25 | 191 |
| Chapter 26 | 199 |
| Chapter 27 | 203 |
| Chapter 28 | 207 |
| Chapter 29 | 213 |
| Chapter 30 | 217 |
| Chapter 31 | 228 |
| Chapter 32 | 239 |

| | |
|---|---|
| Chapter 33 | 249 |
| Chapter 34 | 255 |
| Epilogue | 265 |
| *Free Books* | 269 |
| *Please Leave A Review* | 271 |
| *Books By Ned Marcus* | 273 |
| *About the Author* | 275 |
| *Acknowledgments* | 277 |

# 1

Pale orange snow fell over London, and it flurried around Luke Lee as he cycled into Smith Square. The colour of the snow was only the first of three things that were odd.

The second was that he, a psychologist and linguist, was about to meet the home secretary.

The third was the reason for that meeting.

An old church dominated the centre of the square, and tall trees, barren of leaves but covered in fairy lights, inclined towards it. Dickens had called St John's a petrified monster with its legs in the air. Now, the monster was orange.

Leander Amis's home was one of the restrained Georgian buildings around the edges of the square—the one with the blue front door. Luke was nervous about the meeting, not least because he was unsure whether he could help. He leant his bike against the railings near a grey van. It should be safe; it was old and battered—not the best choice for a thief.

He walked up to the building, taking his mask off when

he reached the porch. There'd been a warning not to ingest the strange snow, which he'd been careful not to do, and he imagined it accounted for the lack of people—most people now commuted even short distances by car. His wife wanted him to reconsider his habit of riding everywhere, too, but he believed a mask was enough protection.

He knocked loudly.

The door opened slightly, and he thought he heard someone speaking inside.

"Hello?"

There was silence. It seemed that whoever had opened the door had just disappeared. He wondered if everything was alright. On an impulse, he pushed the door open wider. Inside there was a darkened hallway with a small table to one side. He listened.

Thinking he heard someone, he said, "Mr Amis?"

Still no one answered. He'd only communicated with Leander Amis's assistant and had not yet met the man. The assistant had stressed the home secretary's security arrangements, so he was surprised by the absence of the police guard. He waited, wondering if he should call the assistant again.

Then, noticing a large envelope on a table with what looked like his name on it, he pushed the door wider still. Perhaps Amis had left it for him. Shaking off his discomfort, Luke stepped into the hallway and picked it up. It was addressed to him. It appeared to contain documents, but, not feeling comfortable just taking it, he put it back.

A shadow moved in a room at the end of the hallway.

"Hello?"

It was late Friday afternoon, and the light was fading. He couldn't see anybody, but when he heard his name he walked down the passage towards the partially open door.

Voices came from the room—it sounded as if Amis was replaying the audio of the strange language he'd sent Luke. Intruders had been recorded at his country home speaking an unknown foreign language. It was the reason he was here. He pushed the door to the room fully open.

The room was large, with hundreds of books lining the walls. In the right-hand corner of the library was a circular stairway with a brass bannister leading down to a lower level. Two lamps lit the room, assisted by the remains of the daylight coming in from the three large windows facing the garden. Orange snow flurried around them. One of the windows was partitioned off with a set of ornate Japanese screens, each portraying geishas amongst cherry blossoms. Luke imagined that Amis had created a secluded personal reading area.

"Luke." The voice came from behind the screen.

It was Leander Amis. Now confident, Luke walked to the screen and gently pulled it back.

He gasped, his stomach turning heavy and cold.

Leander Amis lay naked on a rich rug, and blood trickled from his mouth. His hands were nailed to the floor, and around him knelt four hooded, chanting figures.

They spoke the strange language.

As the last of the daylight disappeared, the room darkened, and a faint green light flickered and jumped around the figures' fingers as Amis slowly writhed. A howling came from the figures that made Luke's legs shake. He blinked several times, no longer feeling in full control of his body. Although he prided himself on his clear thinking, his thoughts became fuzzy. Feeling disoriented, he edged backwards. One of the figures looked up at him, but because of the lack of light, all Luke could see was darkness beneath the hood. He reached for the screen for support.

Amis opened his eyes and saw Luke. He tried to speak, but only blood came out of his mouth. And then he went still. Luke knew that he'd be dead, too, if he didn't get out of here fast. The threads of green light jumping between the dark figures and the corpse were fading. Another of the figures, a woman, screamed, sending shivers down Luke's spine. And something responded. A scratching sound came from the cellar.

Luke staggered across the room, glancing at the circular staircase. An orange light flashed, reflecting on the brass bannisters. Something was climbing the stairs, and a burning smell entered the room. Luke reached for the doorknob, but his hand was shaking so much that he had problems getting a grip on it. On the third attempt, he managed to close his hand around it but almost lost his grip when he saw a black panther at the top of the stairs. Its head was the same height as his chest. It watched him with bright orange eyes.

Fire bubbled around its mouth.

He stared at it, feeling confused by what he was seeing. The panther snarled. Then it moved. Hardly able to breathe, his hand fumbled with the doorknob again, and this time it turned. Luke almost fell backwards through the door. As he did, he saw a man in black behind the panther. He slammed the door shut behind him and ran down the hallway, grabbing the envelope from the table as he passed. As he ran out of the front door, the library door swung open, and the panther rushed down the hall.

He slammed the front door shut, cursing when it bounced back open. The lock was broken. His bicycle was still there. He stumbled down the steps onto the now foggy street and cycled unsteadily towards the main road. At least the snow had stopped falling.

As he turned the corner, he glanced back, seeing the panther's bright eyes watching him. The man in black walked to the grey van, but the panther was still, and Luke breathed out a sigh of relief. But when the engine started, the panther hurtled towards him.

Close to panic, Luke raced into the moving traffic, hardly looking and hardly noticing the blasts of car horns.

2
———

The grey van trailed him.

Only five cars separated them as Luke raced through the thick fog towards Lambeth Bridge. He welcomed the fog, hoping it would hide him, but he realised that it didn't only help him. The panther blended perfectly into the foggy night.

Luke wanted nothing more than to be at home. He'd planned to get home early to see Molly. She was pregnant, and their child was due in the next few days. But this nightmare had stolen his happiness. He had to lose the monsters.

Ignoring more horn blasts from irritated drivers, he forced his bicycle onto the roundabout. One man wound his window down and stuck his head out, but Luke was gone and could only hear the rushing wind. He didn't care if the police stopped him; he'd welcome it, but he hoped to see his wife first. But no one stopped him for breaking traffic regulations, and seconds later he rushed onto the bridge, deciding at the last minute to stick to the road and not ride on the pavement. Even a small delay in lifting his bike over the barrier was too much. What he'd witnessed was so serious that he was sure the police would soon be searching for him. They were certain to have record of his appointment at the home secretary's house. But how could he explain what he'd seen without being considered insane or a liar?

Distracted, Luke hit the car in front. His bike slipped from under him, and he slid along the road. Ignoring scratches, he scrambled to his feet and ran back to his bike. Jumping on it, he pedalled past the car as the driver shouted. But Luke was racing for his life. He considered his options. He knew the backstreets of Kennington well, and as long as he could stay on his bike, he had a chance of escaping.

He raced off the bridge, towards the Imperial War Museum, but before reaching it, he took a sharp right onto a smaller street. Risking a look behind, he was relieved to see nothing but fog. He passed a few pedestrians, but everyone had their heads down and masks on as they walked into the cold wind.

He was now in Kennington, closer to home, and he seemed to have lost the grey van. He'd not seen the panther since crossing Lambeth Bridge. He started breathing more easily and took the most direct route home, but he stopped two streets from his house, just in case they were still following him. He waited.

After several minutes had passed and nothing appeared, he continued on his journey. Soon he was cycling up the alley behind his house. Pushing open the gate, he dropped the bike in the snow. His could see his wife in the kitchen; she had the small red-and-orange baby sweater she was knitting for their son in her hands. He rushed inside, slamming the door behind him and locking it.

Molly looked up in shock. "Luke! What's happened?"

He realised the clothes he'd worn to meet the home secretary were no longer so smart. He closed the blinds.

"Luke? What's wrong? You're acting strange."

"I was attacked."

When he'd finished explaining his story, she hugged him, but he knew she didn't really know what to make of what he'd just said. She brewed a pot of tea and took a packet of biscuits from a cupboard. The meal he'd planned to buy on the way home hadn't happened.

For the next few hours he recounted, in more detail, what had happened, answering her many questions. He needed to calm down before calling the police.

"Do you think you might be a suspect?" Molly asked.

He shook his head. "Impossible." But when he thought about it, he realised there was a possibility that they might suspect him. "I'll just explain what happened."

"It seems so incredible," she said.

In the comfort of his home, even he was doubting some of the details of what had happened. Leander Amis's library had been dimly lit, and he questioned whether he'd really seen light flickering around the hooded figures. But the murder and the panther were real.

"I think you should call the police now," she said. She went to check the back door.

When she came back, he moved closer to her. He felt the baby move.

"He's strong," she said.

He nodded. "Once I call the police, I'll be questioned . . . It might take some time."

She smiled. "I may have a few days; I can spare you for a couple of hours."

With a feeling of dread, Luke telephoned the police. He had to describe what had happened several times. Finally, he was put through to a serious-sounding officer, who listened quietly.

"Dr Lee. Don't leave your house. We'll be there shortly. You'll have to accompany us to the police station."

Luke hung up. "They'll be here soon."

She put the sweater on the table and took his hand. "Come upstairs."

"What?"

"I just want to show you something." He followed her upstairs and into their bedroom.

"Close the curtains," he said. He was still uneasy after the chase.

"No one can see us—and we're not doing anything." She reached into a bag next to the window radiator. "Look!" She proudly held up a tiny red-and-orange knitted hat. "It'll match the sweater. Do you like it?"

"It's wonderful." He felt lucky that he'd met Molly, and he didn't want anything to spoil the birth of their son.

"Really?"

"Yes, really." He knew she was fishing for compliments, but he didn't care. "It's suits him."

Molly laughed. "How do you know? He's not born yet." Then her mood changed, and she frowned. "You don't like it; I can see."

Luke stared at a dark shadow on the window behind her, not understanding what he was seeing.

"What's wrong? If you don't like it, I can knit another."

She sounded hurt, but he didn't take his eyes away from the shadow. "Get away from the window."

"Luke?"

A pair of orange eyes stared at him. He was too terrified to move in case he caused the thing to attack. "Just do it!"

When she didn't move, he said, "Molly." He tried to keep his voice calm. "Step towards me."

"Luke, you're acting strange. This is not like you."

Heart racing, he looked to her, making certain not to shift his head. There was a look of hurt and concern in her eyes.

The panther mewled like a cat.

"What's that?" Molly turned and screamed as the window collapsed inwards. Its mouth closed around her arm.

Luke ran at it and punched its mouth. He felt a sharp pain and wetness, but forgot it as the creature ran down the outer wall, dragging his wife with it—the tiny woollen hat still in her hand.

"Molly!" Luke screamed, pushing his head out of the broken window. The panther pulled his wife over the snowy garden. He considered jumping.

"No!" she screamed.

The back gate opened, and the figure in black walked in. The grey van was parked in the alley behind his house. Luke looked around for a weapon, then he remembered the knives in the kitchen. He sprinted downstairs, taking three steps at a time. When he got to the kitchen, he reached for a large knife hanging from a hook, then screamed in pain. He looked at his hand in confusion; it took several seconds before he realised the end of his left ring finger was missing —his wedding ring with it.

Refusing to allow shock to incapacitate him, he took the knife and tried to open the door again, almost stabbing himself when it refused to open.

Molly screamed from the garden.

One-handed, he pulled on the door again, before realising that Molly had bolted the back door to be extra safe.

Trembling and close to panic, he fumbled one-handed with the bolt before finally flinging the door open and running outside, expecting to fight the panther. But the animal was gone.

"Luke!" Molly was in the alley behind the row of houses.

The man in black punched his wife, threw her into the back of the van, locked the door, and then rushed around the vehicle towards the open driver's door.

Luke charged at the passenger door; he had no time to run to the far side of the van. He pulled the handle, but pain from the bloody stump on his hand paralysed him. The man put the van in gear as Luke used his other hand to work the handle. The door was locked. The man, his face hard to see in the darkness, turned to him and pointed into the back, toward Molly, and then made a cutting gesture across his throat. There was just enough light for Luke to make out a tattoo of an angel on his throat.

The tyres span in the snow, and the van shot forward along the alley. Luke grabbed hold of the handle but slipped to the ground. Struggling up, he ran back into the garden and grabbed his bike as the van drove away.

"What's happening back there?" his neighbour shouted.

Luke looked up to see the top of his neighbour's head over the fence separating their back gardens. He'd hardly ever spoken to the man, and he had no time to explain what was happening. But he hesitated when he saw flames coming from his bedroom. The panther was staring down from the window. It must have gone back for him.

It began to crawl down the outside wall.

"Get inside!" Luke shouted.

But when the neighbour peered over the fence and saw Luke with his bloody hands and clothes, and the knife in one hand, he cursed.

"I'm calling the police!" the man said.

"Fine. Do it inside!"

The panther ran along the outside of the wall onto the section belonging to his neighbour. Luke had no idea how it stuck to the wall, but it did. It then launched itself. Luke rushed from the back garden with his bike. The van had already reached the end of the alley. He leapt back on his bike and pedalled as hard as he could.

From behind he heard a scream. There was nothing he could do. He had to get to Molly. He followed the grey van, but something landed in the snow behind him, and he felt a searing pain in his right leg. Half turning, he saw fire coming from the creature's mouth. He pedalled harder and rushed out of the alley and onto the street, accelerating after the van. He hurtled down the road, not caring about the car sliding towards him with brakes on and horn blaring. The driver opened his window, but the giant panther hit the car, sending it onto the pavement.

Luke ignored the cries from behind. And for most part, he hardly felt the pain from his finger and leg. His dread of losing Molly overwhelmed all his other concerns.

# 3

Ruth Hardy put the phone down, realising she may need a new boyfriend. She didn't like to lie, but what could she do. Not even her parents knew what she did.

She sipped her coffee.

She didn't really blame him; after all, no sane person would cancel a date to work late on Friday night writing reports for a food technology company. The company and occupation were fictitious. Ironically, she spent her life searching for the truth.

Ruth worked deep within MI5, one of the most secretive security services in the world, and that evening, her job was a matter of national security. As a biologist in the newly formed biological and chemical warfare unit, her job was to assess biological threats to the nation. Although originally trained in zoology and botany, she now specialised in microbiology. The orange snow, and the sickness reported in central and south London, and in part of Cheshire, were now her concern. There were fears the sickness was manmade, and that it was somehow related to the snow.

The restricted geographical occurrence of the snow

confused her. The illness, which she didn't believe to be very serious, mostly consisting of rashes, nausea, and vomiting, was even more localised. The area around Shakerley Mere in Cheshire had the most cases, followed by Battersea in south London. This made no sense to her.

Like everyone at Thames House, she was shocked by the murder of the home secretary. It'd only happened a few hours ago, and the police were already searching for the murderer. But few people at MI5 knew that Shakerley Manor, his Cheshire home, was located at the centre of one of the only two places where orange snow had fallen. His London home was within the other area, although not at its centre. She turned her mind back to biology.

Putting her empty mug on the desk, she looked again at the sample of orange snow through her microscope. It puzzled her. The colour came from particles of sand, and this was partly made up of fragments of tiny crustaceans. The problem was, the crustaceans were proving impossible to identify. They appeared similar to some known varieties, but also quite alien. However, she didn't think crustaceans that had died thousands of years ago were causing the illness. She'd also found traces of fungi that could be causing a problem. Derek White, a chemist and the head of the unit, walked into the lab.

"Found anything?"

She nodded. "But it doesn't make sense."

"What exactly?"

"The crustaceans I've found are unlike anything I've ever seen, and now I've found spores of a desert fungi in the samples."

"In London?"

"I know," she said.

"Could it cause the sickness?"

"I think so, but I need to run some checks. The only fungi like this comes from the southern parts of the United States, and it causes something called valley fever."

"And you think that's what the people are suffering from?" Derek asked.

"Something like it."

"How serious is it?"

"If this is a biological weapon, it's not very effective. For most people there are hardly any symptoms, but for some there's a loss of smell, rashes, nausea, and vomiting."

"Is it contagious?" he asked.

She shook her head. "I don't think it's very dangerous, but what's strange is that these specimens are different from anything I've seen. They have unusually high concentrations of mitochondria."

"So they use a lot of energy?"

She nodded.

"But how can snow contain the spores of a desert fungi? And why is this particular snow only falling in Cheshire and London?" he asked.

"Good question—"

His phone rang, and Ruth looked through her microscope again. The cell walls looked different, too.

"Ruth?"

She looked up. The tone of his voice had changed, and she knew he was going to ask her something she wasn't going to like. "What?"

"An outside job."

"Now?"

She'd already cancelled her date and settled in for a long evening, but in the comfort of her lab, not going out to do fieldwork.

"I'm afraid so. You're needed at Leander Amis's country estate in Cheshire."

"What?" she asked, feeling confused. "What could I do there?"

"The snow around his estate is a deeper orange than in London. It keeps changing colour."

"Can't you just bring the samples here? This is one of the best-equipped labs in the world." She really didn't want to drive up north, especially not in this weather.

He shook his head. "The snow's falling very heavily, and it appears to be changing its texture and colour every few hours. We'd be sending back samples all the time; we think it's better that you're there on the ground. You'll need to set up a field lab.

"A helicopter will leave in an hour; we have a driver ready to take you."

"So I'm supposed to spend the night alone in an old manor?" Her evening was getting worse.

"You're the only qualified person available, and we want you to begin work as soon as possible. We need to know for sure whether someone is testing chemical or biological weapons in the area. It may be a coincidence that this is happening at Amis's country home. We don't know yet. The police are there to search for any leads relating to the murder, so you won't be alone."

Her heart sank. The more she thought about the snow, the less likely it seemed to her to be any kind of biological weapon. It was just odd. But she had a personal bag, plus a field lab contained in a second larger bag, ready for situations like this, which were thankfully rare.

"I'll be ready in twenty minutes."

An hour later she was flying up north. She'd messaged her boyfriend to try and calm the situation, only to receive an angry response, and then a second angry response ending their brief relationship. She was twenty-seven years old—too old for this. At least when she'd gone out with Jack, an intelligence officer in MI5, she could be honest. He'd always understood because the same thing happened to him—even more frequently. That had been part of the problem. She'd wanted to be able to see him more often than his job allowed. She should have just accepted him for what he was, instead of pushing him to get a job with regular hours like hers. He just wasn't suited to a desk job, even one in MI5.

The pilots didn't speak. They had enough to do to concentrate on flying through the snow, and she was the only passenger, so she thought about the murder and the orange snow, feeling frustrated because she could see no logical link between the two. Eventually, her thoughts drifted back to the last time she'd been to Cheshire. The memories were bittersweet.

Jack lived in Holmes Chapel, not far from the manor, when he wasn't in London. She knew he might be sent there in the morning, and she considered calling him but immediately rejected the thought. She was nervous about how he'd react. Their last call had been difficult. At least there would be police there. The idea of spending the night alone in an empty manor was extremely unappealing.

The helicopter rattled loudly, making her grip her seat. She'd always wondered, with all the shaking, how they managed to stay in one piece. It didn't help that she'd once read an article explaining that for every hour in the air, they needed between twelve and twenty hours of maintenance. She was basically sitting in a vibrating box with a tendency to pull itself apart. The sooner she landed, the better.

Nothing was visible through the windows, and although

the snow had stopped, it'd been replaced by fog. The manor had been built on a headland extending into Shakerley Mere, a lake that had formed in an old sandpit, although the composition of the sand inside the snow was different from that of the mere.

"We're coming in to land," a pilot said.

She waited. A few minutes later, a light flared beneath them. Ruth closed her eyes and prayed, starting when they landed with a bump. A minute later the door opened, and a local constable helped her with her bags. He was a boy of about nineteen and seemed very young to her. He took the heavier bag that contained her field microscope and other equipment; she carried her personal bag. The pilots wanted to leave immediately, and minutes later they took off. She glanced at her watch. It was almost ten o'clock; she still had time to take some samples and examine them before going to sleep.

She shivered in the cold wind as she followed the constable to the manor. It was so quiet compared to London. He led her to a library with large windows that overlooked the garden. This room alone was bigger than the whole of her flat in London. A long wooden table sat in the middle, and a desk faced one of the three large windows with a view of the mere. Although she couldn't see them, she knew there were two islands.

"You can put the bag here," she said. She'd hoped for a more private place to work. Compared to her lab deep inside Thames House, this place, with its vast windows, felt exposed. But she doubted that anyone would be wandering around the grounds of the manor, especially not in this weather.

"Wait till you see this," the constable said.

He took out a book from one of the bookshelves and

then reached inside and pulled something. He stepped back when the bookshelf opened, revealing a hidden room. There were a table and chairs inside.

"A secret library. I've heard the manor has secret passages, too, but I've not found any," he said.

"How did you find this room?" she asked.

"It was open when we came in. Do you want to use it?"

He seemed excited by the idea of using a secret room, and she let him put her bag on the table and turn on the table lamp. The smaller room made her feel more comfortable anyway. He pointed to a lever at the back of the bookshelf.

"You can shut the door if you want." He then left her to unpack.

Even the hidden library was bigger than her bedroom in London, and apart from the table and wooden chair, it had two leather armchairs separated by a small table. She imagined a couple of glasses of port placed there and discussions late into the night. Leander Amis had been known as a wine connoisseur.

The walls of the inner library were also covered with bookshelves and yet more books. One of them was particularly thick and had a single word printed on the spine: "Poussez." She pushed, but it was stiff. She pushed harder, and a narrow piece of the bookshelf creaked and slowly opened. She stuck her head inside. It was pitch-black and smelt musty. It didn't look as if Amis had used these passages for a long time, if ever.

It was dirty, and she didn't feel like going inside, but she was curious whether it led to another secret room. Although learning more about the crime was Jack's department, perhaps she could help. Taking her torch out, she shone it inside. It would mean getting dirty, but she had a change of clothes in her bag. Ruth stepped inside and found the passages formed a T shape. The library was at the left end of the T, near a narrow set of stairs, which were cramped and dirty. The right end stopped abruptly. It smelt of coal. The longer part of the passage ran past the dining room and ended with a lever in the wooden wall. She pulled the lever and stepped out into the hallway. Leaving it slightly ajar, she walked back into the library, feeling pleased with herself for finding the passages so soon. The young constable either hadn't learnt French or hadn't been observant enough.

About ten minutes later, she'd set up her field microscope on the table. It was sturdy and good enough for most work, although not nearly as powerful as the microscopes in Thames House. She placed her boxes of slides, coverslips, and other equipment within easy reach. Now all she needed was to collect samples of the snow. There was a lot outside, and she decided it'd be best to collect some samples immediately and examine them before sleeping.

A sound came from the other side of the bookshelf. She opened the concealed door; it was the constable.

"Do you need any help?"

"No, I'm fine. I'm going outside to collect some samples."

"In the dark?"

"There's a full moon, and I have a torch. Have you found anything interesting here?"

He shook his head. "Not really." He paused. "It's a bit strange that the intruders broke in but didn't take anything, at least, as far as we know. They left the valuables, and they didn't touch Amis's collection of shotguns." He pointed at an oak cupboard near the corner. "Oh, and we've heard sounds outside."

"Sounds?" She was now a little concerned.

He grinned, and she wasn't sure whether he was joking.

He looked like a boy at that moment. "Some dogs were barking earlier."

At his words, her shoulders relaxed. She hadn't realised that she'd tensed to begin with. "I can deal with dogs, and I'm not going too far." He still stood there, looking a little embarrassed. "What?"

"We need to go now. Are you okay here alone?"

Ruth was annoyed, but she was used to sudden changes. In one way she was relieved. She didn't particularly like the idea of this boy walking into her room by accident during the night. But the idea of being alone in an old manor house in the countryside didn't appeal to her either. Still, if the most dangerous thing here was the odd dog, it wasn't too bad.

"I'm fine."

Ten minutes later as she watched them get into their police van, the older of the two constables spoke to her. "You can use any of the bedrooms upstairs." She nodded, and then they were gone, leaving her standing alone in the porch facing the circular driveway. She breathed in the fresh air. It was silent, and if there had been dogs there, she couldn't hear them now.

In fact, the mere was surprisingly quiet, and no sound at all came from the nearby motorway. It was half past ten, which she realised was late for the countryside, and most people would be inside. But she wasn't tired, only uncomfortable from the helicopter flight, and she decided to take a short walk and collect her samples on the way. She slung a bag over her shoulder and picked out a walking stick from the rack in the hall in case there really were dogs there.

The fresh air in her face felt good. Woodland lay on either side, although to her right, she could see the water beyond. Her new gloves and scarf kept her warm, and the torch she'd brought was powerful enough to see the path clearly, although she hardly needed it with the moonlight. The snow lay undisturbed on the path, and hers were the only footprints. Stopping where there was a space between the trees to her right, she walked to the edge of the mere and shone her torch towards the smaller island. All she could make out was the shape of the ruined tower in the darkness.

Stepping back onto the path, she continued walking. The woods became thicker and darker, but she could still see the path with the moonlight. Further ahead, the snow was darker, perhaps a deeper orange. Her sample would come from there.

The path narrowed, and the trees seemed to push closer to her. Although she knew that no one would be there, she wondered whether her decision to walk through the woods at night had been wise. Telling herself that the manor was too isolated and the weather too bad for anyone to be there didn't help. The atmosphere had changed now she could no longer see the lights of the manor house.

A branch snapped in the trees—Ruth froze in place on the path, gripping the walking stick. She waited but heard nothing. Nervously, she shone her torch into the trees. Perhaps it'd been her imagination, but she'd never considered herself to have an overactive imagination, unlike a few of her friends. Surely no one would be in the woods on any night, let alone on a night like this.

Jack had often commended her on a calmness that she wasn't feeling at the moment. She breathed deeply, thinking of her kick-boxing skills, which gave her confidence. She told herself that it was just an animal and continued walking.

Just as she thought it, she noticed animal tracks crossing her path. She stopped in shock. Feeling her legs weakening, she leant heavily on the walking stick. She knew a lot about animals, but these tracks were unlike anything she'd ever seen. Each print measured around fifteen inches. They came from the trees near the mere and went into the woods to her left. Controlling her breathing as best she could, she studied the tracks, trying to imagine the animal that had made them. It walked on two legs, and each of the five toes ended in a large claw. Whatever it was appeared to drag a long tail behind it. Shakily, she shone her torch into the woods. Something moved again.

This was impossible. There were no animals like this. Some local children must be playing a practical joke; they must have made the tracks. She was about to call out to whoever it was playing the joke, but something stopped her. What if it wasn't a joke? Remembering the strange animal reported near the suspect's house in London, she backed up along the path, keeping her torch shining on the wood and repeatedly telling herself that the tracks were impossible—it must be a trick.

Slipping out her mobile phone, she whispered, "Jack." The phone began to call him. All her worries about speaking to him had gone. She wanted him here right now. She just hoped he'd answer; their last conversation had been short and blunt.

"Ruth, I don't want—"

"Shut up!" she whispered.

"What?" She felt his irritation rising—ready for an argument.

"I'm in trouble."

His tone changed. "What's wrong?"

"I'm at Shakerley. By the mere." She heard it move again.

"Outside?"

"Yes." She hesitated, realising how ridiculous this would seem. "Jack, something's stalking me."

"Get back to the manor and lock yourself inside. I'm on my way." She heard him moving around his flat.

"What about the snow?" she whispered, worried about him riding his bike in this weather.

"Just stopped." She heard the door shut behind him.

"It's an animal," she said.

"A dog?"

"No." She described what she'd seen.

"It could be children playing a trick. I used to do that—"

"I remember you telling me, but the tracks come straight from the lake. Jack, I'm scared." She was already walking quickly, looking over her shoulder as she went.

"I'll be there in half an hour."

She walked faster, not wanting to run. She knew dogs would chase someone running from them. *Be confident*, she told herself as she turned a circle with her torch held tight to check that nothing had come from the trees. Something splashed in the lake, and she almost fell on the slippery path. When another branch snapped, she sprinted as fast as she could. The manor was clearly visible with the porch light on.

She slipped on the icy path, her torch rolling under some bushes. Without stopping to pick it up, she ran inside, slamming the door shut and bolting it.

## 4

Visibly shaking, she rushed into the kitchen and shut the small upper window. Peering through the larger window onto the driveway in front of the house, she relaxed a little. It was snowing again, but nothing was moving. She closed the blinds and then went from room to room closing the curtains and turning the lights on. If anything was outside, she didn't want it watching her movements nor knowing which room she was in.

Ruth returned to the library, which was the only room without any curtains or blinds. Nervously, she looked through the large french windows into a dark garden that ran down to the lake. At least there was an ornate Japanese screen hiding the entrance to the small library. She re-entered it and put her bag on the table. She had no intention of going outside again tonight; she'd collect the snow in the morning.

Wondering what to do, she looked more closely at the books, shivering as she read the spines. Through the Gates of Death was the first in a row of occult books. She didn't believe in this stuff and was surprised someone as distinguished as Leander Amis had, but they did disturb her. She decided to ignore them, but then she noticed a diary stuffed deep between two other books, and she pulled it out. It was handwritten and consisted of notes of daily events around the manor. She flicked through it but found nothing of interest. It seemed to be mostly Amis's notes on his estates. He noted a drop in the numbers of fish in the mere, but nothing else caught her attention.

Deciding she needed a coffee, she walked back through the main library, purposely ignoring the large windows facing the mere. She was more comfortable when she reached the kitchen. At least no one could watch her from outside. She put the kettle on, then glimpsed through the blinds again. It was just after eleven o'clock and Jack would be here soon. She was worried about him riding a motorbike through the snow, knowing how fast he liked to ride.

The snow was falling harder, and the tracks she'd seen would be covered soon. Jack was so down to earth that he wouldn't believe the prints were real unless he saw them himself. But what if he was right and it was children. Inventive children could have made the prints, but she would have expected to see their footprints, too, unless the snow had already covered them. Perhaps they'd made them a few hours ago. That would be more reasonable; it was late now, so they'd have gone home.

She heard a sound from the drive, but the boiling kettle distracted her. She quickly made two coffees, relieved that Jack had arrived. The sound was clearer now; he must have raced here through the snow to get here so quickly. She shook her head, smiling at his rush to come and protect her.

"Wait a minute. I've locked the door!"

Putting the steaming mugs of coffee on the kitchen table, she walked down the hallway to the front door. Quickly opening the door, she shivered as a blast of cold wind blew inside. She froze. The driveway was empty. Nothing moved. Her fear suddenly returned, and almost falling back inside, she slammed the door shut.

Her skin crept as she returned to the kitchen and peered through the blinds again. *It must be the wind*, she thought. But then she noticed that the trees were still. Snow fell from one of the larger trees, and she breathed out in relief. Of course, it was a snowfall. Taking her mug of coffee, she walked back into the library, glancing at the french windows as she passed. She was determined to prove to herself that nothing was there. Was she so used to the city that a bit of countryside scared her?

Then she heard a sound again.

Convincing herself it was just a sound of the countryside, she forced herself to walk up to the large french window. She sipped the steaming coffee. Something moved, and her heart leapt. Then she laughed, and putting the coffee on the floor, she opened the french window, not caring when snow blew inside.

"Are you cold?"

A dog stared up at her. It looked like a retriever sheepdog mix.

"It's okay. Do you want to come inside?"

Having a dog inside would give her comfort, and it seemed friendly. It sniffed her hand but then turned and trotted towards the row of bushes along the left side of the garden. She closed the window. Despite her relief, her legs felt wobbly. Now she regretted calling Jack. He'd just laugh at her. Perhaps the dog belonged to the children who had made the tracks.

About fifteen minutes later, she heard Jack's motorbike —the sound was familiar from their rides through the countryside. He banged on the front door, and Ruth ran through the house, opening the door in relief. She hugged him tightly.

"Ruth, are you okay?"

"I am now. It was just a dog." She told him what had happened.

"It's most likely just children out late playing with their dog," he said. "I used to be out late when I was a boy."

She knew about his past and his particular reasons for avoiding returning home until his parents were asleep or out of the house.

"I made a coffee for you, but it might be cold now."

"I like cold coffee."

She laughed. "I dropped my torch in these bushes. Can you see it?"

Jack crouched down and looked into the bushes. "Where?"

"In front of you."

"There's nothing here."

She went outside and crouched down next to him but couldn't see her torch. "It was here. I dropped it when I thought I heard something coming; the light was still on."

"Perhaps it rolled further than you thought," Jack said.

The bushes were thick, so it could have rolled further. They went inside, and she showed him the hidden library.

When he looked at the titles on the spines of the books, his eyes widened. "I'm not surprised you've been feeling nervous surrounded by books like this. Have you collected your samples yet?"

She shook her head.

"But you found something strange in London?"

Although he was investigating a possible terrorist involvement in the murder of Leander Amis, it was unusual that the orange snow was concentrated around his property, so she knew he would have read her reports. "Yes, but I can't make much sense of it. Not yet. All I know is that the sand in the snow shouldn't be there, and that some of the things in it are unlike anything I've seen. One of the microorganisms is new."

"A new species?"

She nodded. "Finding a new species isn't that strange—new species are discovered all the time, but there's no reason that something like this should appear in London."

"And here?"

"That's what I'm here to find out."

The dog barked outside. "It's coming from where I found the footprints," Ruth said. The barking became more intense.

"Something's upset it," Jack said. "Perhaps I should check." He took a large torch from his backpack. She wrapped her scarf around her neck to follow, but he paused at the front door. "I want you to stay here."

"I don't want to be alone." He started to protest. "It's probably just children." She gestured in the direction of the barking dog. "You said so yourself."

He hesitated.

"There are shotguns in a cupboard in the living room."

"Loaded?"

She shrugged. "I don't know. Maybe we could find some bullets."

"Cartridges." He grinned. "But it's probably nothing. Bad guys don't like hanging around in freezing cold weather in the middle of the night." They listened. "It's stopped now."

"I'm coming. I feel safer with you," she said.

He nodded, and they left the house together.

They walked back along the path; her footprints had

disappeared under a fresh layer of snow. About ten yards ahead of them, the dog growled.

"Something's really upsetting it," he said.

It yelped, and then there was silence. They ran towards it.

"My torch," Ruth said, spotting the light just off the path. "The dog must have dropped it here." She picked it up and ran to catch up with Jack. She stopped and muffled a scream, moving closer to Jack for his warmth and safety. The dog's head lay in the snow on the path.

"Jack?" She was terrified. "What did this?"

Jack stared at the head. "The cut's clean. I don't know any animal that could do this. A sword . . ."

"Or a claw," Ruth said. "I can't see any human prints."

He frowned. "But the force it would need . . ." He looked towards the trees on the right. "The prints go straight into the trees by the mere."

"It's gone back," she said. She shone her torch on them.

He bent down to examine them. "There're no animals this size in the country. I can't see a tail."

"It might have lifted it," she said.

He took out his phone and videoed the scene, and then he stepped closer to the trees surrounding the mere.

"Jack! You're not going in there?"

His previous training in the special forces had made him tougher than anyone she knew—her kick-boxing skills were a joke compared to what he could do—but she was still nervous.

"Shine your torch into the trees," he said. "Two lights are better than one."

She did, but she didn't like it when he pushed aside a branch. "There's nothing here." Stepping inside the trees, he disappeared from sight.

Ruth followed him; she had no intention of being left alone on the dark path. The wooded area was narrow and led directly to the water. She stared out across the mere but couldn't see anything except the dark tower on the island.

"Look," he said quietly, pointing to the snow. The set of tracks disappeared into the mere.

"Jack, I want to go inside."

## 5

Trying to keep the grey van in his sight, Luke ran a set of red lights, fractionally missing a speeding car as he raced onto the main road. To his left was Kennington Park, and ahead and to the right was the Oval cricket ground. He paid no attention to the curses and horn blasts, but he felt his heartbeat racing as the van sped further away.

A car drove alongside him, and a man opened the window and shouted, but to look was to lose time. Luke's stomach sank as the van grew smaller in the distance. He raced in the direction of Clapham. The road rage driver followed, blasting his horn. Glancing to his left, Luke noticed a shadow running through Kennington Park.

He pedalled harder.

Then the traffic lights turned red, and the man stopped, apparently ready to launch another round of insults. Luke adjusted the kitchen knife in his belt. The man fell silent when he saw the knife. He averted his eyes and quickly closed the window.

Feeling more comfortable, Luke rode through the lights and continued to race towards Clapham Common. The grey van was becoming hard to see clearly. It seemed to hesitate, as if the driver wasn't sure where he was going, and then it moved forward, passing the Tube, and turning right by Clapham Common.

A police siren sounded behind him, but stopping meant losing the van. Reaching Molly was all that mattered. The police pulled alongside and pointed to the side of the road. Even if a murderer hadn't kidnapped Molly, he probably wouldn't have stopped, not with the panther moving through the deserted streets. It was further back but keeping pace with him.

The police turned on their siren for a few seconds and tried to cut him off, but he mounted the pavement, forcing pedestrians to dive out of his way, and raced towards the junction where the van had turned. It was moving towards Battersea Power Station, perhaps back towards Smith Square. Then he lost sight of it, but the police still followed, overtaking him as he approached the junction.

He had to decide what to do. Would surrendering help Molly? And what about the thing following him? Clapham Common was ahead, and he swung right at the junction, almost losing control of his bike, then continued north; the Common was now to his left. He decided the police could wait. He'd ride in the direction the van had gone, but first he had to lose the police. He decided to cut through the Common, then cycle back towards Battersea in the hope of finding the van there.

The police did a U-turn in the middle of the road and were in pursuit again, this time with the siren on full. Pedestrians stared at the desperate cyclist rushing from the flashing lights of the police car. He'd almost reached the north corner of the Common when the police cut in front of him again. He mounted the pavement, riding through a group of men. One of them swung a punch but missed and slipped on the icy pavement. Luke smelt alcohol as he rushed past them and then back onto the road. He was now on the north side of the Common. Again the police car cut in front of him, but this time the police didn't hesitate. They drove right up onto the pavement. Luke swung left, skidding to a stop in front of the barrier. He swung the bike over and continued to ride, hoping that the darkness and fog would hide him because there wasn't a lot of cover otherwise. He realised the pain from his wounds, and from losing Molly, had affected his judgement, but he'd made his decision and he'd stick to it.

The police pursued on foot, and he guessed that they'd send cars along some of the lanes that crisscrossed the Common. He had no idea whether they'd recognised him and wanted him for questioning about the murder of the home secretary, or whether this was just about breaking traffic regulations.

A man stumbled from some bushes, walking straight into the bicycle. Luke flew from the bike, hitting the ground and rolling over. The snow only partially softened his fall, and he felt the skin leave his hands and arms. He grunted at the pain in his finger. Standing and checking his body, he watched three angry men approaching him. One wore a hoodie, while the others wore woollen hats pulled down over their ears.

Normally he'd have been nervous—he was no fighter—but losing Molly had changed everything. He didn't care about them, only about the delay they caused.

"Watch where you're going!" the man in the hoodie said.

Luke picked up his bike.

"Is something wrong with you?" the man continued. "Can't you hear?"

Luke paid no attention to the man—he'd heard someone approaching. It could be the police. He tried to ride the bike, but the wheel was twisted. He got off and tried to straighten it. The man said something and lurched towards him. Luke pulled out the knife, and the man backed off.

"We're all friends here," the man said, raising his arms.

But Luke saw one of them reach into his pocket. Possibly he had a knife. He threw the broken bike at the nearest man and sprinted. They followed, but running through the snow was hard, and soon they were struggling. His fitness from riding his bike every day was his advantage. He left them behind and was about to loop round to Mount Pond when he saw another man running towards him. Unsure who he was, Luke changed direction and ran directly towards the main road.

A snarl came from the fog, followed by a scream. He wasn't sorry. They were giving him time. He also had the advantage of knowing the park. Luke ran towards the pub near the main road. Police whistles came from behind, but there was no sign of the panther. At last he reached the main road, wondering what to do next. He seldom hesitated over decisions, but he was beginning to feel overwhelmed. Should he surrender to the police or continue his search for Molly? No longer knowing what the best thing to do was, he stood on the pavement.

Perhaps it was a noise that alerted him; he wasn't sure. He turned round, wishing he'd surrendered to the police. A pair of orange eyes watched him from the darkness.

# 6

Amelia Blake drove home through the fog after a hard day at the hospital. There were days when she questioned her career choice, and today was one of them. She liked being a nurse, but she knew she didn't want to still be doing this in ten years. Then she thought about the three years she'd spent as a rally driver. She'd been good, but not good enough. She realised that all her choices were really ways of delaying the choice she most wanted, but she couldn't see how to make it work.

Her higher calling was something she seldom spoke about because of the reactions it provoked. The devoutly religious feared the devil, and nonbelievers belittled anything spiritual. But there were people who did believe. And to deny her calling would be to deny who she was. Her psychic skills were a part of her. She understood that people who lacked this sense, or who had been too lazy to develop it, thought she was either stupid and irrational or a charlatan, but she couldn't help that. She felt it was her duty to use her skills. Exactly what form that might take, she hadn't decided.

Her colleagues had suggested she take public transport because of the weather, but she was confident she could handle her car, a red Mini Cooper, like one she'd once raced. The pale orange snow did worry her, though. Not because it made driving any harder than regular snow. Nor because of its strangeness, nor the theories of environmental degradation that were spreading on social media. Nor even the rumour that the orange snow and sickness were related. If they were, she didn't think it serious. She'd dealt with a few cases of rashes and nausea that were possibly caused by the snow. The strange snow worried her because of a dream she'd had each night for the past three nights.

The dream had repeated itself exactly, and she believed that repeated dreams had significance, but these were far more intense than normal, making her think the significance was deeper. And this morning, when she'd been working at the hospital, she'd had a vision. Although no one had noticed, she was still shaken by the experience.

The vision had been the same as the dreams in every detail, except for the ending. In each dream, orange snow fell, but when it touched the ground it caught fire, and she found herself in a burning city. In her dreams she'd woken at that point. But at the end of the vision this morning, she'd seen someone watching her—someone with bright orange eyes. If she'd not been so busy at work, she'd have contacted her spirit guides. She now had two days off, and she needed the rest. Tomorrow morning, the first thing she'd do would be to make contact with her guides on the inner planes. But first she needed a good night's sleep.

Amelia was almost home and really looking forward to a hot shower, something to eat, and bed. She was tempted to skip dinner, but a small snack was probably a good idea.

Then everything changed.

As she peered out of the fogged-up windscreen, she had a strange feeling. Her heart sank, but she listened carefully. As she slowed her car, she felt an increasing sense of urgency.

Something was about to happen.

She believed in following her intuition—it had served her well—but when she had a sudden feeling that it was best to drive straight ahead instead of turning left towards her home, she almost ignored it. It was cold and foggy, and all she wanted was to go home.

But after making mistakes earlier in her life, she'd made a decision to always follow her intuition. She'd developed it to a point far beyond normal, and it was there for a purpose. Sighing, she continued to drive straight ahead, by the Common, rather than turn down Elms Road, where she lived. As she passed her turning, she saw a long line of red lights. Feeling sudden relief, she smiled to herself. She was being too dramatic. Her intuition was simply advising her not to get caught in a traffic jam. She decided to take a longer loop and enter from the other end of the road. That way she'd avoid the congestion, which was only on one side of the road.

She drove slowly through the fog, pleased that this stretch of the road was quiet. Then a movement on the opposite side of the road caught her attention. A man rushed from Clapham Common. He stopped on the pavement looking lost. Something was wrong.

She pulled over and waited. Was this the reason her intuition was speaking to her? The man appeared agitated. Something moved behind him, and her eyes widened when a black panther walked from the darkness.

*"HELP HIM!"*

Amelia jumped in her seat. She had feelings, intuitions, and knowings, but she seldom literally heard a voice, but now her inner voice was screaming. She shuddered, putting her car in first gear. It looked in her direction, and a deep feeling of unease passed through her. Its eyes glimmered in the dark.

*"NOW!"*

She accelerated across the road.

"Get in!" she shouted through the open window as she slid into the kerb, making the man jump back. The animal was moving fast towards him. He ran around the front of the car, opened the passenger door, and jumped in.

"Go!" he yelled as the panther leapt into the air.

It was much bigger than she'd thought. She accelerated, but it hit the side of her car as she pulled away, propelling her into the left-hand lane.

"Faster!" he shouted.

"I know." She glanced at him and noticed blood on his shirt and a knife in his belt. She accelerated and started sliding towards a streetlight, gaining control just in time to veer away. Seeing the flashing police lights in her rear-view mirror, she debated whether to stop, but her instinct was to keep going. She followed her instinct.

"You're not stopping for the police?"

"Do you want me to?" she asked.

He shook his head. "I need to go towards Battersea Power Station."

"Well, you can do that yourself. I need to get away from that thing. What is it?"

"A sort of panther."

"Sort of?" She glanced at him—his face was red from the cold. She noticed his bloody fingers. "It did that?"

"They've kidnapped my wife. I have to find her." He didn't look at her. She wondered if he was in shock.

"Your wife's been kidnapped?"

She was unsure what to think. She couldn't deny her intuition, not when it screamed at her. Nor could she deny that the panther-like creature chasing them had bright orange eyes. He turned round to look; she glanced back through the rear-view mirror. It was catching up. She threw the car around the corner and accelerated again.

"Why did you stop?"

"It looked like you had a problem."

"Many," the man said.

"Your wife and the thing trying to kill you."

"The police are after me, too."

Shaking her head, she wondered what she had got into. She wasn't sure if the time was right to ask more details; she was still trying to get away from the weird creature.

"Will you help me?"

"I am in case you didn't notice," she said.

"I need to find a grey van that's driving towards Battersea Park."

"I saw you run from the park." She accelerated past a car. "When did you last see the van?"

He was quiet for a few moments. "Half an hour..."

"Then it's gone."

"I have to find it." He was becoming more subdued.

"To find your wife?"

"And child."

She looked quickly at him and saw a mix of anger and resignation in his eyes, before turning back to the road.

"She's pregnant; the baby's due any day now."

Amelia understood why her intuition had screamed at

her. This man had a lot of problems, and the panther suggested that they were not normal ones.

"You need to call the police," she said, "but first you need to get your hand sorted."

He seemed to see her for the first time. "Who are you?" he asked.

"My name's Amelia Blake. I'm a nurse."

"I'm Luke Lee."

She drove fast, took a sharp turn left, accelerating out of the bend.

"Are you a rally driver, too?" he asked. His eyes focussed on the tiny rally car key fob dancing under the ignition.

"In another life."

He lapsed into silence, and she concentrated on driving. For a moment she thought the car was going to slide, but it held. The creature slid round the corner behind her, but she was pulling away.

"It's fast," she said.

He gave a curt nod, and she glanced at him. He was in his early thirties, a little older than her, and would have been well dressed if his clothes hadn't been in tatters.

"What's happened to your leg?"

"It breathes fire," he said.

He appeared serious. "How can it do that?" she asked.

"I've no idea."

She raced straight through a set of red traffic lights, only just missing a car, but the creature wasn't so lucky, and it was knocked across the road. Further back she could see police lights. But she was faster; she had no intention of stopping with a creature like that chasing her, not even for the police.

He turned to her. "Where are we going?"

She raced through the next set of traffic lights and seemed to lose it. At least, she couldn't see it through the fog.

"Away from that thing."

She turned a sharp left onto Elms Road. The line of slow-moving traffic was still moving slowly. Turning left again, she drove into a driveway. A garage door opened automatically, and seconds later the door was closing behind them.

"You seem more together than just a passer-by," he said.

She looked at the blood dripping into the interior of her car. "I'm many things. Let's look at your hand first. We can go inside and speak."

The strength of the messages that she'd received told her this was serious. A kidnapped wife was bad enough, but it was something the police could deal with. She had a feeling, though, that something about this may be beyond the police, and she might have to become more deeply involved than she'd like.

She needed help from the inner planes.

7
---

Amelia listened to Luke's story, feeling more and more uncomfortable.

"What did the killers look like?" she asked, quickly washing his wound. It was lucky his fingers were numb; most had already turned white. He hardly flinched.

"They wore hoods. A green light flickered around their fingers." Then he shook his head. "Perhaps I imagined that."

As he spoke, she finished stitching a flap of skin hanging from his missing finger over the end.

"Why were you at the home secretary's house?"

"To help with a translation of a recording of criminals who'd broken into his country home. I've been working on a new device with a group of colleagues that translates languages. It's a hobby, really."

"And he wanted you to translate the audio?" she asked.

"Yes. I'm a psychologist, but I have training in linguistics, too. The language is very unusual, and I think our device could help. At least, it'd make things faster."

"Are the police aware of this?"

He shrugged. "I called them when I got home. I told

them about the murder, but I don't know if they know about the device."

"Do you know which language they were speaking?" she asked.

"I've got no idea."

"I need to look at your leg." His trousers were burnt, and she carefully cut them away from the knee. At least his leg hadn't been badly burnt. "I have some cream for this." He breathed more easily when she applied it.

Amelia didn't know much about this type of magic, no one did. From Luke's description, she guessed they'd been using Amis's vital energy to perform magical work, which was the real reason behind ancient blood sacrifices, but she had no idea what type of magical work it might be.

When she finished, they sat at the kitchen table. He looked up at a picture of a rally car racing through the snow.

"You were serious about being a rally driver," he said.

"I came fourth in the Rally of the Thousand Lakes."

"Thousand Lakes?"

"The World Rally Championship in Finland," she said.

"No wonder you're good on ice."

He went quiet. Attempting to distract him, she asked about the panther.

He shook his head. "How can a fire-breathing panther be prowling the streets of London?"

"Good question." She glanced at the kitchen clock. It was eight thirty. "Let's watch the news."

A reporter stood outside Leander Amis's house in Smith Square.

"Home Secretary Leander Amis has been murdered in his Westminster home. His assistant and a police officer guarding his home have also been brutally killed and their bodies dismembered.

"A thirty-four-year-old professor, Dr Luke Lee, is the prime suspect, although police suspect that others were involved."

He was only two years older than her.

Luke sat up straight. "I'm innocent!"

The cameras cut to the scene of a burning house in Kennington. Luke's jaw dropped. His shock appeared genuine.

"My house."

The newscaster continued. "His neighbour's dismembered body has been found in his back garden. The killing appears senseless brutality. Dr Lee's wife has also gone missing."

Amelia thought through her choices. The news story claimed that Luke Lee was a dangerous criminal, but her inner voice had spoken differently, and that was not something to take lightly. And then there was the fire-breathing panther. She knew she'd follow her intuition, as she'd long ago chosen to do. But she wanted answers.

The newscaster paused for breath. "The suspect, Dr Lee, a noted psychologist, who was seen running from the house covered in blood, has left a trail of death in his path. His fingerprints have been found on Amis's body."

"Impossible," Luke said. "I didn't touch him."

She looked at his bandaged stump. "Who has the end of your finger?"

He went pale. "They took my finger..."

"Someone must have visited your house after you left," she said.

She took a bottle of white rum from the fridge and poured two glasses. She seldom drank, but it seemed appropriate. He took the glass without comment.

The list of killings continued.

"Shortly after the murder of the home secretary, Dr Stuart Baker, a top linguist who was working with Dr Lee, was brutally murdered."

Luke gasped as an image of Baker appeared on the TV. "He was my friend."

"It's believed that Dr Baker was working on a secret project with Lee, related to the home secretary."

"Of course he was!" Luke said loudly. "He was part of our group."

"How could the killers have found him?" Amelia asked.

"Amis had the full list of people involved in the project."

The news continued. "Two police officers in pursuit of Lee were brutally slashed to death on Clapham Common, and two members of the public were also seriously injured."

Luke now sat with his head in his hands.

"Under no circumstances should the suspect be approached. He is armed and extremely dangerous. There's a report that he's accompanied by a dangerous animal. If you see this man, call the police immediately.

"Reports coming in from Clapham Common also suggest Dr Lee has an accomplice. The police are searching house to house in the area. Anyone having seen a red Mini Cooper driving at high speed from the Common in the past hour is urged to call the police immediately."

Amelia turned the TV off. She was involved whether she liked it or not.

"I'm innocent," he repeated.

"If I didn't believe you, I'd call the police."

She thought about the green light and decided to be direct. The sooner he understood her, the better. He'd just have to deal with it as best he could.

"Do you believe in magic?"

He looked at her with wild eyes. "What?"

"What you described sounds like a black magic ritual to gather etheric energy."

Luke glanced at the tarot cards on the table before looking back to her. "What do you mean?"

She put her empty glass down on the table. "I study the occult."

"Do you know where Molly is?"

She saw hope in his eyes disappear as she shook her head.

"What's happening is very serious," she began.

"I know! They've kidnapped my wife!"

"It may be worse—"

His voice rose. "My wife's been kidnapped—how much worse can it get?"

She could imagine many ways, but she wished she'd chosen her words more carefully. She really did fear something worse. She remained quiet, allowing him to calm down.

After a moment, Luke's anger seemed to deflate. "So you think the light was magic?" he asked.

"A form of energy."

"Why would they take my wife?"

The answer wouldn't make him happy, and she hesitated to say it. She could be quite blunt sometimes.

"Tell me," he said.

"A pregnant woman has more of this energy."

"So they want to feed?"

She shook her head. "Something else."

"What?"

She wished she knew. "Perhaps we can find out."

He'd taken her revelation calmly. Then he pulled a large envelope from his jacket. "I'd almost forgotten. I found this in Amis's house." With his good hand, he put it on the table.

"Help me open it."

Amelia pulled it towards her. "It looks like he wrote your name in a hurry," she said.

"It might have been the last thing he wrote."

She opened the envelope and pulled out four sheets of paper; three had images printed on them. Shakerley Manor was written on the front of one of them. She spread them out on the table. They showed a series of strange symbols; they'd been taken from a book.

Picking one up, she peered closely at the image. "They look like magical symbols, but I don't recognise them. Those seem different." She pointed at some other characters.

He pulled them closer with his good hand. "It might be the written script of their language."

"Does it mean anything to you?" she asked.

"No. There's not much I can do with it at the moment. I need to get a device from one of the members of our group. That may help with the spoken language."

"Don't you have one?" she asked.

"I did before my house burnt down. There were five, but now there're only three left. I think Stewart's house is off limits."

"If you get one of these devices, can you identify it?"

"I don't know." He shrugged. "Do you know how many languages there are in the world?"

"I've got no idea," Amelia said. She'd never thought about it.

"About seven thousand spoken languages. Three or four thousand of them have a written script."

"And your device can recognise them all?"

"More than any other software."

Amelia looked at the magical symbols. Some of the symbols were familiar but had an exotic differentness about them, but some were unlike anything she'd ever seen.

"So we have two languages here: a magical one and a linguistic one."

Luke nodded. "I want to get one of the devices before I call the police. With that news report, I think I need to collect any evidence indicating my innocence. "

"Where's Shakerley Manor?" Amelia asked.

"Somewhere in Cheshire. If I can identify the language, I'll have something to give them, and a way of helping them find Molly." He seemed to be talking more to himself.

She unfolded the letter, and her jaw dropped open as she read.

"The home secretary was involved in the occult," she said.

Luke shook his head. "I'm not completely surprised."

She read the letter aloud.

"'Our country is facing an existential threat. A magical assault has been launched against us . . .'" She felt the blood drain from her face as she wondered who the real Leander Amis was. He was hated by half the country, but she doubted if anyone suspected this. She read more. "'These people have a far deeper knowledge of magic than I do.' He might have written this while captive in his own house," she said.

"That would make sense."

Amelia continued to read aloud.

"'Here are pictures I took of pages of a book I found in the grounds of Shakerley. The symbols have magical and mundane meanings. I've only been able to understand a little. It's important you know that they're beyond criminal. They're abhorrent. Their magic is pure evil.

"'I have reason to believe that they are planning to

commit an atrocity in our country at sunrise on Sunday, 23rd December—'"

"The day after tomorrow," Luke interrupted.

She nodded and continued. "'I wish I understood their true intentions, and why I've been targeted. I hardly think it's because of my part-time interest in the occult.

"'I do know that it's imperative they're stopped.

"'Your life is in danger. Keep this letter as proof of your innocence if anything happens to me.

"'As the Home Secretary of the United Kingdom, I have full trust in the police force of our country, but this matter is beyond their capability. You must remain at liberty until Sunday morning. Identifying and translating the language is crucial. I am profoundly sorry for having involved you in this.

"'Unfortunately, the police will be unable to protect you from the methods these people use.'"

Amelia chilled as she glanced ahead at the next paragraph.

"'Someone will contact you. It's been arranged from the inner planes. Follow her instructions on anything magical, but use your own instincts, too. Ask her to reach out to the inner planes for assistance—'" The letter ended abruptly.

"Is this real?" Luke asked.

She shivered, passing it to Luke. The meaning was clear. She'd already been contacted and instructed to help this man. She was already involved. And the police were not the answer—not yet.

"It looks like he had no more time." She felt stunned and poured two more glasses of white rum.

"Are you this person?" Luke asked.

She took a sip of white rum as she tried to calm herself. She had no doubt about it.

"Were you contacted from the inner planes?"

She nodded and told him about the message she'd received as she'd driven home.

"A voice?" Luke took a sip, pulling a face as he drank it.

"Usually it's more subtle." She watched his expression: hope mingled with uncertainty.

"Can you help?"

"I can try." She pushed the half-empty glass away; she wanted a clear head. "I need to contact my guides..."

He sat back and stared at her. "Guides?"

"Spirit guides." She sensed silent dismissal. She was a natural empath; she felt the emotions of others, and she often knew their thoughts, too. She'd always found it frustrating when people denied thoughts and feelings she could literally feel. But she didn't blame them. After all, most people believed their thoughts and inner emotions were private. As a child, she'd not understood that others couldn't sense what she could; her gift had hurt her many times.

"If I'm to help you, then you need to understand that some of my methods are unconventional."

He nodded politely, but he was still withdrawn.

"It's important you don't dismiss what you don't understand, especially at this time."

Brows furrowed, he looked at her, considering. At least he was now listening.

"This conversation is strange," he said.

She smiled. "You're not the first to say that. I'm going to visit the inner planes. I need you to be quiet for several minutes."

He nodded, and she looked at him sternly. "That means don't speak to me!"

He pulled the pictures towards him and began to study them.

# 8

Amelia needed to be calm to contact her guides, but calm was the last thing she felt. She closed her eyes, and breathing from her stomach, she tried to relax. Slowly, she entered a meditative state and called her spirit guides.

Her kitchen faded from sight.

She was in the desert; this was one of several places where she met her guides, but something was different. She looked around, searching for them. She had six, but she was alone, and the heat was unusually oppressive. She waited, but the ominous feeling remained. She noticed a darkness moving towards her. Waiting for a few more minutes, she made out a sandstorm.

Preparing to return to the physical world, she slowly backed away, but the orange storm slowed, stopping in front of her.

*"Victoria?"*

Victoria was her chief guide, the one she'd had since she'd been a child, and the one who understood her the best. Amelia had always welcomed her warmth and unconditional love. But she couldn't see her.

Instead, a dark figure stepped from the swirling sand. He scared her.

*"Who are you?"*

*"I am Viktor; I'm the new leader of your guides."*

*"Victoria is my head guide."*

Although she didn't say it, she also considered Ernest and Teal as the second tier of leadership.

*"I'm a temporary guide,"* he said. *"I'm here to help you with the special problems you're now facing."*

*"Where's Victoria?"*

*"Here."* Victoria appeared from the blowing sand; the stern Ernest and the fierce Teal were by her side.

*"Who's this?"* Amelia asked, indicating Viktor.

*"He's the warrior chief you need to stay alive,"* Victoria said.

This comment sobered Amelia. *"What's happened?"*

*"There's a threat to life on Earth,"* Ernest said. He gestured to the growing orange storm blowing around them.

Amelia listened intently, hoping this had nothing to do with what she'd just experienced in London, but she knew it did. Viktor stepped forward, and with her three closest guides standing there in the desert, her confidence returned.

*"An orange storm threatens to engulf your world,"* Viktor said. *"It must be stopped."*

*"What if we can't?"* Amelia asked. She didn't see how she could deal with something so serious.

*"The storm will spread. Recall your vision!"*

Amelia instantly remembered, and the repeated vision of a burning Earth almost overwhelmed her. All around her London burnt; the screams were sickening.

*"An orange wasteland will cover your world."*

She saw the bleak orange wastes before her. Amelia was

now very concerned. She realised she was breathing too rapidly.

"*And worse . . .*"

"How can it be worse?"

"*You only see a small part of a larger storm. Workers on other worlds have slowed its advance, but if unchecked, it will envelop your world. It must be opposed.*"

Centring her breathing, Amelia calmed herself. "*It's already started in London, hasn't it?*"

The remaining guides materialised before her, joining her new guide. They were dressed as magicians and now sat in a semicircle on ornate chairs—the sombre Viktor sat in the centre, flanked by Teal and Victoria. She felt as if she were petitioning for favours at some exotic medieval court. But they were so serious. She shivered despite the heat and waited for them to continue. Ernest, the guide who seldom spoke and seldom smiled, spoke next.

"*What is happening is bigger than this man and his family. Passively surrendering to circumstances will guarantee your death and that of many others. You have little time and must act, regardless of the desires of mundane authority.*"

Now Amelia was listening intently. She knew that mundane authority was his way of saying the police.

"*The real danger,*" Ernest said, "*is not the enemy themselves, nor the murders they commit. It's what they'll allow into your world if they succeed in opening a permanent portal.*"

"What kind of things?"

"*Life of another order inhabits the gaps between universes. It's dangerous. Eventually it would find its way through. This is the greater danger. The lesser is that invaders from their world would conquer yours.*"

"Lesser?" It sounded catastrophic.

"*There'd be hundreds of millions of deaths, and most animals would disappear from your world, but they'd give advances in science and technology beyond the imagination of most people."*

"Hundreds of millions dying sounds pretty bad."

*"I said it was the lesser danger."* Ernest looked the most serious he'd ever looked. He continued before she could speak. *"If this were all that were to happen, then in a few centuries, humanity would mostly have forgotten."*

This was harsh, but probably true. But now she was concerned about the second danger.

*"You're right to worry,"* Ernest said, reading her mind. *"Even the enemy, despite their advanced knowledge, are unaware of the danger that lurks in the spaces between the universes. That which would enter would not be easy to remove."*

"Talk about pressure," Amelia said. The images of her guides flickered when she almost lost control and returned to her kitchen with Luke. *"What can I do?"*

When she regained control, Viktor spoke. *"They'll attempt to open a portal to their world. Stop them. And at all costs, stop them from using it."*

*"How?"*

*"Communicate this to others who will help you. But first, you need to learn more. Visit the Akashic Library . . ."*

Hearing her guides was becoming difficult.

She thought about the Akashic Library. This was a library of sorts—a place where every thought, feeling, and action that had ever occurred was recorded within the fabric of the universe itself. She'd visited it before, but finding the right information in the vast vaults of the Akashic records could take multiple lifetimes, and she wasn't even sure what information she needed.

Amelia's eyes opened wide, and she felt her breathing becoming unsteady as their concern washed over her.

*"I have to know more. Is there anything else you can tell me?"*

*"Two things,"* Viktor said. *"First, they're aware of you and will attempt to kill you."*

Amelia was sweating despite feeling a deep chill. She was having difficulty breathing, which she needed to control to maintain contact with her guides. *"And second?"*

Viktor leant forward and his mouth opened, but she felt a disturbance. Her vision of the guides faded. Something shook her.

She opened her eyes.

"You're on the news!" Luke said. "I thought you'd want to see."

Amelia felt like slapping him but was too disoriented to do anything.

"I told you not to disturb me! Never do that again! I was speaking to my guides."

He raised his eyebrows and then pointed at the TV.

Coming back like that disoriented her. And it was dangerous, but she knew he couldn't understand. Trying to focus her eyes, she saw a picture of herself on TV. She wondered where they'd got it from. The reporter continued. "She's believed to be an accomplice in the chain of murders running from Westminster to south London. It's believed she lives in the vicinity of Clapham Common."

She knew she was in this deeply. It was as her guides had said.

"We must leave immediately," she said.

"The Security Service is now involved in the investigation," the reporter continued.

"MI5," Luke said.

The news then switched back to the mysterious orange snow and to the sickness affecting people living in the areas where it had fallen.

She turned the TV off. "I think we should follow

Leander Amis's advice. We need to discover some things for ourselves."

"We?"

"You saw the news. I'm committed, whether I like it or not. And I'm not sure the police could protect us anyway. Something bigger is happening."

Luke nodded. "I think you're right; the police can't protect us. And they may slow my search for Molly." Then he nodded again as if finally committing. "I must do what's best for her."

Something screamed outside, and Amelia started, sending her glass to the floor. She watched the fragments of glass spread out across the tile floor as if in slow motion.

She looked at the window, wishing she'd pulled down the blinds. But it was too dark to see anything, apart from the snow falling near the window.

"Perhaps it's just a cat fight," she said.

Luke stood and shook his head nervously. "There's something in your garden."

She joined him and peered through the window into the darkness beyond.

Two bright orange eyes stared back.

## 9

Irritated, Ruth ended her call to MI5. "They told me to get some sleep."

Jack put his phone away.

"The same," he said. "They're not interested in animal tracks."

"But they're real."

He nodded.

"What do you think made them? You don't still think they were made by children, do you?"

He shook his head. "There's something there. The tracks were real, and no child would have the strength to kill an animal like that." Jack glanced around the room. "Show me the shotguns."

She led him into the living room and opened a cupboard behind a leather armchair. There were four double-barrelled shotguns. Jack took them out and opened them at the breech. The barrels were clean.

"Looks like he was a sportsman."

He passed her one of the shotguns and put two of them

back. There were several boxes of cartridges at the bottom of the cupboard.

"I still have to collect snow samples."

"Tomorrow," he said. "I'll sleep in the—"

"We can use one of the bedrooms," she interrupted, pulling him closer.

"What about—?" Jack began.

She knew he was remembering the last time they'd spoken. "I was wrong. Do what you think's best with your life." He held her. "I want you with me tonight," she said, glancing at the clock on the wall. It was almost midnight. Not late for her, but she didn't want to sit in the library with a shotgun in her lap. "Let's go to bed."

They found a bedroom, and Ruth bolted the door. It wouldn't stop someone serious on getting in, but it should make entering noisy enough to wake them up. She placed the shotguns on the floor next to the bed. Then she took his hand.

Several hours later, Ruth woke up. She sat up straight in bed and felt Jack wake up next to her. It was still dark. "I heard something."

"Ruth?" His arm moved around her waist. "We're in the countryside. The sounds are different from the city."

"I know that." She got up and looked out of the window. It had stopped snowing. A thick fog hung over the lake, and the light of the full moon diffused through it. "It's five o'clock."

"Ruth, it's too early."

"I heard something," she insisted. She turned on a bedside lamp and picked one of the shotguns up. "We need to check."

He leant over, turned the lamp off, then got up. She could just make out his naked body.

"Have you become shy?" She grinned in the darkness.

"If there's someone downstairs, I want my eyes to be adjusted to the dark."

She stopped smiling, feeling anxious again. They silently dressed.

"Do you think it's the thing that killed the dog?" The prints in the snow seemed less real now.

"I don't think it's anything, but if the killers have come back, I want to be prepared."

She nodded. "There are secret passages. I found an entrance inside the hidden library." She described what she'd seen.

"I'd rather be in the open," Jack said. "We have two guns and plenty of cartridges."

She felt her jacket pocket, which was now full of cartridges that Jack had insisted she stuff inside. That was something she wouldn't have thought to do. He was silent as he walked ahead of her along the landing, stopping at the top of the stairs. They'd left a couple of lights on; one was sending a dim light into hallway beneath them. Jack pointed at the second step down and then shook his finger in warning. The tread had creaked on the way up. Carefully stepping over it, she followed him downstairs.

In the hallway, he froze. She was about to speak, but he put a finger to her lips, silencing her. She looked around, unable to see anything wrong. Then she noticed that the door to the dining room was open; it'd been closed the night before.

They stood next to one of the entrances to the secret passage, and she fingered it, but he shook his head. She gently opened it anyway. But Jack was calm. She guessed that he would be with his training. So when he suddenly backed out of the dining room, pushing her backwards, she became more nervous.

*"What?"* she mouthed silently.

He pointed, and she froze.

A shadow stood motionless in the room, except for its tail, which twitched. Ruth tried to control her breathing. It tilted its head, and she slipped into the secret passage.

"Jack!" she whispered.

The shadow moved like lightning, but Jack was fast, too, firing both barrels. It ripped the gun from his hands. Apart from a hiss, it hardly reacted to the shot. Jack backed into the secret passage, and she pulled him in quicker. Its head seemed to expand, and something hit the other side of the panelling after Jack slammed it shut. She pulled him deeper into the narrow passage. The acrid smell was intense, and the wooden panelling next to his head was smoking.

"It spits acid," Jack said.

Ruth was already moving down the passage, pulling Jack with her, when it smashed into the narrow entrance, breaking the panelling. It was a lizard. A type that shouldn't exist. Its head pushed into the passage, but it was too big to fit inside. She led Jack in the direction of the secret library.

"I still have a gun," she said.

"I'm not sure it'll make any difference. I shot it with both barrels, and it hardly noticed."

It watched them move away. Then it vanished.

"It's gone." She breathed out in relief and edged along the passage.

"Quiet," Jack whispered. Then he pushed her forward, and she stumbled.

"Jack!"

A claw cut through the wooden panelling where she'd been. It was in the dining room.

"Run!" he shouted.

It ripped away the panelling that made up one of the walls of the passage, separating them. "Go!" Jack shouted. She moved deeper into the passage, but when it stretched an arm towards Jack, she rushed back and shot it in the head. It disappeared.

"Jack!"

He ran past the open gap, deeper into the passage. She hugged him.

"Thanks," he said. "You stung it."

Ruth shrieked when its head pushed back into the passage. It reached for Jack again, and they moved further along the passage until they reached the outer wall of the house. She looked back, but it had vanished. "I've not been up the stairs, but left goes to the hidden library," she whispered. "Right goes to a coal bunker. I think it might be an exit. We may be able to get out."

"How do you know?"

"I smelt coal when I explored earlier."

She knew he smiled at her. He always did when she paid attention to small details others ignored. She turned right, and he followed, but then he stopped her.

"What?" she whispered.

He shook his head and whispered in her ear. "It might suspect we'll try to get to the bike. If I'm going to fight that thing in the open, I want more than a shotgun."

Ruth looked at him in confusion. "Jack, are you alright? It's an animal."

"We don't know what it is. And some animals are intelligent. It had the sense to change rooms and break into the passage further ahead. That looks like intelligence to me. In this game, false assumptions kill."

She realised that she knew nothing about it, but she couldn't believe it was intelligent. She'd studied animals all her life, and she'd never met one that could reason in this way. Still, what he'd said worried her.

They listened but couldn't hear anything.

"We should go to the secret library," Jack whispered. "If there's no sign of it, we can leave through the main part of the library. Did you see any boats by the lake?"

"There's a rowing boat at the end of the garden," she said.

"Perfect."

"What about the motorbike?"

"It's snowing. I can't be sure my bike will start straightaway. It's been outside for hours."

He had a point. She didn't want to be sitting on the back of the bike with that thing charging at them.

"Do you have anything in your pockets?" Jack asked.

"Cartridges."

"Anything else?"

"Just this." She pulled out the toothbrush and tube of toothpaste she'd used the night before.

He took them and threw them hard down the right-hand passage.

"Hey!" she whispered.

He quickly put his finger to her mouth. "I'll buy you new ones." He tugged her gently in the other direction, and they entered the secret library.

"Do you really think it heard my toothpaste falling inside the passage?"

He took out the used cartridges and replaced them with new ones. "I don't know."

"Jack?"

"It's got good hearing." He was whispering so quietly that she could hardly hear him.

They waited in the secret library, listening by the entrance to the main library. Jack slowly opened the hidden door and peered into the large room. She checked her watch. It was five forty and still dark apart from the light of the moon. They tiptoed through the library and opened the french window. The house was silent as they left and walked through the fog towards the lake.

The rowing boat was by the water. She'd feared ice, but if anything, the snow was melting. "Get in." She didn't argue. He knew boats better than anyone else she knew. He pushed the boat, and a branch snapped underneath it. He pushed harder, jumping on board.

A screech came from the side of the house—the place near the coal bunker. Jack had been right; it'd been waiting for them there. It must have heard the toothpaste fall after all.

Jack rowed fast, heading straight for the centre of the lake. She sat opposite him with the shotgun in her lap. The creature ran on two legs through the garden and straight into the water. It waded towards them.

"Do you think it can swim?" she asked.

"Yes." He rowed harder.

"Can it . . ." She didn't want to say *catch them*.

"I won every rowing race in the navy; I'm faster than that thing." She wanted to believe him, and perhaps it was true; they'd already pulled well away from the shore.

It stood in five foot of water, watching them. Then it screeched again and dived into the water.

"It's gone."

He shook his head. He was sweating despite the cold wind. He rowed faster.

Then she saw a dark shape moving over the surface towards them. "It's fast—"

"I told you, I'm the fastest." He rowed strongly, deeper into the lake.

She turned round so they both faced backwards. Jack rowed, and she sat watching the dark shape while she clutched the shotgun. It wasn't gaining on them. Jack was good. They passed the small island. The ruined tower loomed out of the fog but was hard to see clearly—just an indistinct shape. It was on the smaller of the two islands.

Eventually, the rowing boat ran up onto the snow-covered shore. They ran straight towards the embankment, reaching it in seconds. Ruth was already shouting into her phone to her superiors at Thames House as she climbed over the fence. Jack watched, shotgun in hand. But nothing emerged from the lake.

They remained on the ridge between the grounds of the manor and the grassy embankment leading down to the motorway.

"What did they say?" Jack asked without taking his eyes from the gloomy lake.

"They're sending a police car to pick us up on the motorway. A few minutes." Ruth watched the area between the mere to the motorway uneasily. "Do you think it's scared?"

"No," Jack said.

"Then why not follow us?"

He shrugged.

She looked out over the water but couldn't see anything in the moonlight. "Jack, what is it?"

"A good question."

"I think it's been here a while," she said.

"Why do you say that?"

"I found one of Amis's diaries. It's mostly just about his

estate, but he complained about a drop in the number of fish."

"That would make sense. It needs to eat like anything else. This can't just be a coincidence," Jack said. "It must be connected with Amis's killers."

"And the orange snow," Ruth said. "It's heaviest here."

He nodded. "If some secret lab in Russia created this monster, they've made incredible advances in genetics. It's something that shouldn't exist. At least, not since the dinosaur age."

She watched his breath as he spoke. "Do you really think it might be intelligent?" she asked. She'd seen films with such creatures. Genetically created dinosaurs. She shivered.

"I don't know. It's an intelligent animal, at least. Some dogs are very smart."

She thought about the dog she'd petted earlier. Then her thoughts shifted to the police car. She wondered how long it'd be. It was early Saturday morning, and there wasn't a lot of traffic. She didn't blame people for wanting to stay home on a weekend like this.

"There!" she said.

She pointed at the blue flashing light approaching along the northbound lane of the motorway.

"It's watching us," Jack said.

She followed the direction of his gaze. "I can't . . ." Stopping in mid-sentence, Ruth saw the dark shape at the edge of the lake about a hundred yards away.

They raced down the embankment to the approaching police car. Ruth almost slipped on the snow in her rush to reach it.

A screech came from the lake.

She hesitated as Jack passed one of the police officers the shotgun.

"Jack?" He looked at her. "The screech came from a different part of the lake."

## 10

The doorbell rang.

Luke hit the light switch, sending the room into darkness. He gasped in pain, again forgetting the bloody stump on his left hand.

The orange eyes had vanished.

"Open the door. This is the police!" They knocked on the front door. "We know you're inside."

Amelia stood by the back door. The only lights were the clock on the oven, the faint glow of the full moon, and a flashing blue light visible through the small frosted windowpane in the back door.

The knocking continued.

Opposite the back door was the side entrance to the garage, but to get into the garage, they'd have to cross the outside path. And on one side were the police, and on the other was the panther, if it was still there.

"We can't stay here," Luke whispered. But he had no idea how they could cross the path without being arrested or killed.

"The next move is theirs," Amelia said. They waited.

"The garage door's unlocked," Amelia whispered, "but the thing's so fast."

A dark shape pushed against the outside of the window. He hardly dared breathe.

"Does the garage door open automatically?" he asked.

She nodded. "But it takes several seconds."

Someone was walking along the path.

"Get back!" Luke shouted.

"He's here!" a police officer called out. A police radio crackled as someone repeated the message. Reinforcements were on the way. "Open the door and come out with your hands up. Both of you."

Neither he nor Amelia replied, and the police officer knocked again on the back door. But a sound in the garden distracted him.

"They're escaping into the garden!" he shouted.

The man ran into the garden, and Luke's warning was drowned by a scream. A second man ran down the path. A shot came from the garden. Amelia unlocked the back door and waited with the car keys in her hand.

The kitchen window imploded, and the panther crashed into the table, fire coming from its mouth. The letter and pictures from the home secretary burst into flames. Amelia shot through the back door and almost fell into the garage door, opening it quickly. Luke glanced back at the panther as it skidded across the kitchen floor, and then slammed the door shut behind him.

More glass smashed.

"It's jumped back out," Amelia said.

She started the car, and the front door of the garage was already opening. Someone stood on the driveway, silhouetted against the flashing blue lights of the police car.

The garage door was taking too long to open.

"Are you ready?" she asked quietly.

"Yes." He glanced at her. "If that's not a police officer, run him over," he said.

"You think it may be the man who kidnapped Molly?"

"I don't know." It was what he wanted and dreaded at the same time.

Snow blew into the garage, and they faced an armed police officer. Behind him a police car blocked the end of the drive.

"Get out of the car!" The police officer pointed his gun at them but kept nervously glancing at the path by the side of the house.

"We have no choice," Luke said.

Then the officer turned and fired at something on the path. Seconds later, flames engulfed the man, and he stumbled down the drive. The panther finished him off; they could do nothing.

As the panther turned to look at them, Luke thought they were finished, but Amelia accelerated, and the car rocketed from the garage straight towards the creature. It backed away, but at the last second, Amelia swerved right, driving through the low wooden fence, onto the neighbour's driveway, and then onto the road. The car slid over black ice before gaining traction on the opposite lane. Something hit the back of the car. Luke looked round to see flames. Amelia accelerated away, with the panther chasing them over the snow. The flames disappeared.

"It's gaining on us," he shouted.

"I know!" Amelia yelled. They flew through a set of red traffic lights, causing cars to slide across the road behind them.

"If the damn thing doesn't kill us, you will!" Luke

shouted. But he grinned when the creature was hit by a car, and they left it behind.

"Where to?" Amelia asked.

"The nearest of my colleagues, Clive. We need one of the devices." He now believed that getting one of the devices was his best way of getting Molly back. He needed to understand what these people were really doing. He looked through the steamed-up window, trying to get his bearings.

"This is Clapham Road," Amelia said.

"He lives near Elephant and Castle."

They drove in silence. Luke thought about the device he'd helped create, and he was confident that if this language belonged to any major language group, then they'd get something on it. Even if it didn't, he hoped they might get some clues. His thoughts were interrupted by Amelia.

"Where exactly?"

"Turn right just after the Tube." Amelia slowed her car. "Here." Three police cars and an ambulance were outside Clive's house. "This doesn't look good."

"Stop or go?"

He wasn't sure what the problem was at Clive's house, and he was about to suggest pulling over on a side lane when he saw smoke coming from his colleague's flat. Medics carried two stretchers from the building.

"Go."

Luke gave Amelia directions to Sue Taylor's house in St Pancras. She was someone he'd known since his university days. Both Sue and himself had chosen to specialise in cognitive psychology.

They sat in silence until they crossed Westminster Bridge.

"Do you think that was related to the murders?" Amelia asked.

"Yes." He couldn't see any other explanation. "They want the device."

She shook her head. "But how would they know about it?"

"From Leander Amis's correspondence."

"Their reaction tells me we really need to get one of the devices," she said.

"It'd be a good start. It's artificially intelligent and learns new languages fast."

"They could already be moving towards her house," Amelia said.

"That's what I'm worried about."

Amelia glanced at him. "Call her!"

"I was worried she'd panic and call the police," he said as he took out his phone.

"If you think her life's in danger, then you have to call her."

She was right. He dialled her number. Her phone rang, but she didn't answer. He shook his head.

"It's quite late," Amelia said.

It was possible she was already in bed, but Luke remembered the late nights they'd spent together when they'd been students. He felt concerned for her safety. Everything was going badly wrong, and he was very aware that everyone he'd come into contact with since the murder, as well as many of his friends, was dead or in danger. He sat in silence, lost in his own thoughts, for the rest of the journey.

"Slow down," he said.

They slowed as they approached the road where Dr Taylor lived. When he saw the flames and the fire engines, he felt as if a weight pressed against his chest.

"Are you okay?" Amelia asked.

He shook his head. "Stop the car."

She pulled into the avenue, and they watched the paramedics bring out two bodies. Luke opened the window and breathed deeply. The cold air helped. The paramedics spoke to the police and shook their heads.

"She's dead."

"You can't be sure," Amelia said.

But he was. As Amelia turned the car around, one of the police officers pointed towards them.

"We may have been spotted," Amelia said. She accelerated away from the crime scene. They drove back towards south London. The last member of the group lived near Guy's Hospital. "We should have gone to this address second," Amelia said.

Luke shook his head. "I've known Sue since university. I had to try and help her first."

The roads were not congested, and the fog helped conceal their car. At least, Luke hoped it did. There was no sign of police pursuit, but he watched the road carefully for any sign of them. He had to warn his last team member of the danger they were in, and to save one of the devices. After that, he didn't care too much if he was caught, but he needed to learn more about these people first. He lost track of time as they drove through the foggy streets.

Dr Martin Harris lived on a lane not far from the hospital.

"Here," he said.

Amelia turned onto the lane. He pressed his head against the front window, trying to see through the fog, and he breathed out in relief. It was quiet.

"Thank God!" he said. He pointed at the house. Amelia turned down a lane and parked the car behind the house.

"We need to be quick," she said.

They got out of the car. Looking up, he saw smoke coming from the second floor window.

## 11

Luke pressed the buzzers one by one. One woman threatened to call the police. No one else answered. His heart raced as he thought through the different options for getting inside. He peered through the window into the ground floor flat; it appeared to be unoccupied.

"If the killers are upstairs . . ." Amelia hesitated. "You know they'll be armed."

"These are my friends. And they have children."

"And the last device," she said.

"That too. But I wouldn't risk my life for it. Or yours." Luke looked around the tiny front garden. He saw a brick.

"But you are," Amelia said.

"I'm hoping they'll think we're the police."

"I don't like it," Amelia said. "The police will be here soon, anyway."

"I'm counting on it," he said.

If they weren't, then his plan could go badly wrong. Luke picked up the brick and threw it at the window. A passer-by stopped and started videoing them on his phone, but Luke no longer cared. Unfortunately the hole was too small, and he spent the next few minutes knocking out enough glass to enter without hurting himself. When he was satisfied, he carefully climbed inside.

"Wait," he said to Amelia.

He ran through the empty flat, into the hallway, and opened the front door for Amelia. They rushed upstairs.

"Here," Luke said.

The door was hot, and smoke was seeping out from underneath it. He stopped and listened. When he was sure there were no sounds coming from inside, he rushed at the door and kicked it repeatedly. Amelia helped, too. Eventually, the smouldering door flew open, and smoke rushed from the flat, making him cough.

"It's toxic," Amelia said.

He had no choice. A police siren came from the street outside, and a minute later the police banged on the door downstairs, but Luke was already in the living room, holding his breath. Martin and his wife lay dead on the floor; their bodies were covered in cuts.

"The panther," she whispered.

Luke nodded. He felt nauseous—not only from the smoke—and rushed to the window, opening it as wide as he could. He gasped for breath. The police shouted something from the street.

"Luke!" Amelia pointed to the sofa.

It moved. Taking his knife out, he slowly pulled the sofa back.

"Uncle Luke," the boy said.

Luke quickly hid the knife. The boy's face was covered in dirt from the smoke and smudged with tears. He was no more than eight and was holding his young sister's hand.

Martin had proudly told Luke only a few weeks ago that his daughter had managed to walk by herself for the first time.

"Tommy," Luke said. "What happened?"

"A black panther." The boy was shaking.

"You and your sister are leaving the flat right now," Luke said.

"But Mummy and Daddy?"

Luke felt sick. He'd made a mistake. Amelia had been right. If he'd come here first, these young children might still have their parents. But it was too late; now they needed him to remain focussed.

"This is my friend Amelia. She'll help you leave the flat."

Amelia picked up the girl and took Tommy by his hand while Luke ran down the hallway towards the study—the place Martin kept the device. The boy started crying. Luke guessed he'd seen his parents lying on the floor. There was nothing he could do. Smoke came from the main bedroom, but the smaller bedroom beside it, and the study to his right, seemed untouched. Luke ran to the study. The two chairs they'd sat in last month, when he and Martin had discussed how their device might change the world, were still there. And the tablet was still on the shelf. He picked it up and left the study.

Amelia ushered the crying children from the flat. They didn't want to leave their parents behind. She had to lift the boy up and put him on the stairwell.

"Get away from those children!" an armed police officer shouted. Amelia left them on the landing and stepped back inside the smoking flat, closing the broken front door as best she could. A sound came from behind them, and Luke saw a shadow prowling across the main bedroom.

"It's come back," Luke whispered.

They rushed into the children's bedroom, and he gently shut the door behind them. With Amelia's help, he pushed the brightly painted wardrobe against it. The police kicked open the flat door, and the panther snarled.

Quickly stepping over toys, Luke opened the window.

"It's too far to jump," she whispered.

He opened a box on the wall and pulled out the fire escape ladder. Martin had once bored him about the protection he'd put in place to make sure his children would be safe in case of a fire. Now he silently thanked him. He threw the portable ladder out of the window.

Shots came from the hallway.

"You first," he said.

Amelia was agile and quickly climbed through the open window onto the ladder. Luke had no idea whether the ladder was designed to hold two people at once, but he had no time to wait. As soon as she was several rungs down, he climbed through the window. Someone shouted something about the panther, but he was too far down to hear. Amelia moved fast, and he was right behind her. At about four feet above the ground, he let go.

"Run!" he said.

The car was parked in a lane behind the house, and they sprinted towards it. More shouts came from the building, but he didn't look back. The car was twenty yards away in the fog.

"They've not found it," Amelia said, grinning.

A movement caught Luke's eye as Amelia unlocked the door with her remote key, and he grabbed her arm, pulling her away.

"What?"

The panther hit the top of the car, belching fire from its

mouth. It turned quickly, snarling at them—its spots glowing orange. More fire dripped from its mouth and smoke rose from the car. Then the roof burst into flames.

"My car!" Amelia cried.

## 12

A sheet of flames roared up from her car.

Feeling shocked, she moved back, away from the intense heat of the fire. Luke was by her side. Surely the panther must be dead. She hoped so; she couldn't see it for the flames. In front of them, a police van slowly edged past the burning car. From behind, a police car approached with its flashing blue lights turned on.

"We're surrounded," she said.

"Almost," Luke said. He glanced at a lane to the right; it led away from the house. "If we run, we can make it." He started to move towards it.

"Wait!" Amelia said. She pointed at a figure standing at the end of the lane. He was watching them, and the feeling he gave off disturbed her. "Do you recognise him?"

Luke shook his head, uncertainly. "I'm not sure. It's too dark to see."

The man disappeared into the darkness.

"Too late anyway," she said.

The police car braked hard, skidding to a stop several yards away, blocking their access to the lane. The driver of the car, a police sergeant, got out. He was speaking on the radio.

Two more armed officers walked from the van. "You're under arrest!" one of them said. "Drop your weapons."

Luke dropped the kitchen knife. "That's all I've got."

"Not good," Amelia said.

The panther walked from the burning wreck. Amelia had to look hard. Smouldering orange spots covered its body. It sent a blast of fire towards the nearest police officer.

"Shoot it!" she yelled.

The officers turned to face it. One of them was shouting for backup. The panther leapt at him. He raised his gun but was too slow, and it cut off several of his fingers. The second officer fired, and the panther chased him back towards the van as he shouted to the van driver for help. It started mauling him, but the officer shot it again, and this time it moved away. The police near the van were now frantically shouting and calling for backup. A second police van stopped behind the first one. Amelia and Luke backed up to the police car. The police sergeant was staring at the scene with a pistol in one hand and a radio in the other.

He glanced at Amelia and Luke. "Stand by the car!" He reached for his handcuffs, but when the panther snarled, he seemed to forget them.

Amelia grabbed Luke's arm and whispered, "Get in." It was a Ford Focus RS, another of the cars she'd raced, and the engine was still running. She got into the driver's seat; Luke sat next to her.

The sergeant fired twice, but it seemed unaffected by the bullets. It was as if its skin was armoured. Other armed officers jumped out of the second van. But before they could do anything, the sergeant walked up to the creature.

"He's gone mad," Luke said.

Her eyes widened as she watched the man. He was taking a huge risk. She put the car in reverse and quietly backed up. She was ready to go, but she didn't want to abandon this officer. If the thing attacked him, she'd ram it with the car.

The panther growled, fire dripping from its mouth. But when it moved, he shot it on its nose. It shrieked, jumping backwards. Police from the second van started shooting, and the injured animal darted around the sergeant and ran towards the man who had been quietly observing from the lane. Satisfied that the officer was safe, Amelia reversed fast, turned, and rushed after the panther.

"That's the man who kidnapped Molly!"

Luke pointed at the man standing in the shadows. He was beckoning the panther. His grey van was parked a little way behind him. The man raised a gun. Amelia cursed, mounted the pavement and drove into him, catching his arm. The gun fell to the ground, and she left the man and the panther behind.

"Stop!" Luke shouted.

But she accelerated.

"He knows where Molly is," Luke said.

"And he's picked his gun up, and he has a deadly animal, and the police may shoot us on sight!" Amelia said.

"I don't care."

"I do."

Another police car was in pursuit. With one foot on the accelerator and the other on the brake, she performed a pendulum turn into the next lane and raced down the side street. Adrenaline rushed through her as she drove as she hadn't done since she'd raced. She braked into the corners with the accelerator on, shifting the car's weight to the front and making the back slide around the snowy bends. Ten minutes later they turned onto a larger but more congested road. For several seconds she studied the switches, and then she tried a few. The siren started, and she overtook everything she could.

"Amelia!"

At least she was taking his mind from Molly. She raced through the red lights, concentrating on the road so much that she hardly heard Luke's shouts or the sounds of police sirens following her. She didn't care. Whatever happened, she was not stopping the car until she reached her destination.

"You'll kill us!" Luke shouted as she accelerated around a corner.

"I'm micromanaging the weight transfer," she said.

Luke raised his eyebrows. "I understand why you didn't stop, but I don't like it. We had a chance to point out to the police who the guilty person was."

"In a battle zone?"

"We could have stopped a little away from him," he said.

"Didn't you see the grey van?"

Luke didn't reply.

"He's fast," Amelia said. "He would have got away, and the police wouldn't have chased a van. Not with us there."

"Perhaps you're right."

"We need somewhere we can go until we decide what to do next," Amelia said. "I know a place. It's near the Common." She paused. "But the people are a bit odd."

"I don't care how odd they are. I just need a place to work and think."

She had questions to ask on the inner planes and needed some space, too. She glanced in the rear-view mirror. "That's not good." A line of police cars with blue lights flashing followed them. "But if you can't beat them . . ." Amelia played with more switches until she found the one for the flashing lights. Then she returned to rally mode as she raced towards Brixton.

"Where are we going?" Luke asked. "I thought your friends lived in Clapham Common."

"A slight change of plan," she said. "Look how many cars are following us." He seemed more stressed than her. "We can't let them follow us there. I know this part of London. We can take a bus from Brixton."

"You're joking?"

She laughed, feeling a relief of tension. "No, actually, I'm not. Don't you think racing a stolen police car with lights flashing and siren on will attract attention?"

"Yes." He raised his eyebrows. "This isn't a subtle plan."

"Nope."

"Look at them all!" he said.

She glanced in the rear-view mirror again. She counted six police cars. "You're right. We need to put more space between us." Accelerating again, a car skidded in front of them, and she dodged around it. Several minutes later they were racing through Brixton. She braked hard and skidded to a stop on Brixton Road. She'd already attracted some of the attention she wanted. A young man started asking them questions.

"Quickly!" she said. "Around the corner before they're close enough to see."

They walked to the corner, leaving the police car with its doors wide open, siren blaring, and lights flashing. It was already attracting a crowd. Further down the road, the line of police cars approached. Turning the corner, they walked to the bus stop. There were only four people in the queue.

"I hope you've got an Oyster card."

"What?" He'd been looking behind them, but her words seemed to bring him back to the present.

She waved her own card in the air. "They don't take cash."

"Amelia, this is insane." But he took out his card anyway. "When does this bus arrive?"

"In two minutes, if it's not late."

"If it is, we're finished."

The police sirens were very close, and Amelia watched the two approaching buses intently, willing one of them to be the No. 35. One of them kept driving towards them.

"Yes," she said.

"You knew the time of the bus?" he asked.

"I sometimes take it."

"What if you'd been wrong?"

"I'd have taken another bus. Lots of them go in a similar direction. We'd just have further to walk."

The red bus stopped, and Amelia jumped on board. Luke was right behind her. As the driver pulled away, two police officers walked around the corner. "Upstairs," she whispered. Although the bus was moving, the police could see inside, apart from where the steps were. By the time she'd slowly climbed the circular stairs, the bus was on its way to Clapham.

"They may call and have it stopped," Luke said.

"Then get ready to run," she said.

It was the most stressful bus journey she'd ever taken. Just over twenty minutes later, she rang the bell.

"Where are we?" he asked.

"Rookery Road."

The stop was by Clapham Common, which was covered in fog.

"Thank God for London weather," she said.

There were few people outside, and the few passers-by didn't even look at the couple walking with their arms around each other. Fifteen minutes later, they disappeared along a side street.

"Do you think it can track us?" she asked.

"I don't know about panthers, but I've heard that bloodhounds can pick up a trail after two weeks. I don't know what this thing can do. And it was shot in the nose."

She grinned. "That was brave of the sergeant."

Amelia led him down a narrow alley and stopped by a dilapidated door leading to a desolate garden. They entered.

"You know this place."

She knew it wasn't a question. Amelia confidently walked up the snow-covered garden path. "My friends are eccentric, but they're the only people I know who won't report us to the police."

Without knocking, she opened the back door and stepped into a warm kitchen.

"Shut the door!" a woman yelled from deeper inside the house.

"The old witch is here!" Amelia grinned.

## 13

Amelia watched Luke stare at the writing on the wall: "Everything the State says is a lie, and everything it has it has stolen."

"Nietzsche," she said.

He raised his eyebrows.

Postcards and pictures with similar messages were stuck randomly around the kitchen. He looked up at the effigies of politicians hanging from the ceiling.

"Can we trust them?" he asked, still staring up at the grotesque figures.

"I think they're the only people we can trust. They don't like the police."

"I can imagine."

A woman in a bright yellow dress walked into the room holding a black cat. It stared at them with eyes that matched the colour of her dress.

"Amelia!" she said. "I'm sorry. I thought it was Dell. He never shuts the door."

"Hannah, I have a favour to ask."

Hannah put the cat on the table and looked into her

eyes. "You're in deep trouble, Amelia," she said, wrinkling her brow. "You're the main story on the news." She looked Luke up and down. "He's the one, isn't he?" Amelia didn't comment, and Hannah led them into the living room.

"Hannah, the situation is more serious than whatever you could have heard on the news."

"Is that possible?"

"Unfortunately, yes. Is everyone here?" Amelia asked.

"Apart from Dell, but he should be back soon."

Amelia looked up at the plastic clock shaped like a black cat. It was just after midnight.

"It's late. I'm sorry."

Hannah shook her head. "No one sleeps early here." There was a sound from the kitchen. "Dell's back." Hannah stuck her head into the hallway and yelled, "Everyone come here! Amelia needs our help!"

A few minutes later, the other three inhabitants of the house had assembled in the living room. Acacia sat next to Hannah, and Dell folded his skinny form onto the armchair. When Rob, the fourth inhabitant, an intent-looking man, brought in mugs of tea, they stopped talking and turned to their guests.

"You assassinated the home secretary!" Dell blurted out.

"This is Dell," Hannah said, looking at Luke. "He's a socialist wizard."

"Social anarchist," Dell retorted.

Amelia had no wish to hear another debate on the relative merits of ideologies and was relieved when Rob interrupted.

"Did you really kill him?"

"No," Luke said, shaking his head.

"Of course not," Dell said with a knowing grin. "And now you need a place to hide."

Luke hesitated, his eyes flicking uncertainly to Amelia. She knew Luke was wondering what he'd got himself into, but her friends were just enthusiastic.

"What happened to your hand?" Acacia asked.

"I was attacked by a panther," Luke said.

Her eyes widened.

Amelia spoke quickly. "Luke, I know these people well; I trust them. The things they believe would shock most people." Acacia grinned. "Complete honesty will save time. They can take it," Amelia said.

"I agree with that," Hannah said, settling comfortably into the settee. "Why don't you tell us what happened?"

Luke went through some of the highlights of the story, and Amelia added details of her visions.

"It wouldn't surprise me if half the Tories were satanists," Dell said.

Acacia giggled.

"Let's listen to Amelia. This is serious," Hannah said.

They quietened, and Amelia continued. "My dreams of an orange storm began before the strange snow and sickness. And they're becoming more urgent. My spirit guides are agitated. This is something much bigger than a string of murders, however horrific."

"Why did they kill Leander Amis?" Dell asked.

Luke shrugged.

Amelia interrupted their questions. "We need a breathing space," she said. "We're being hunted by the police, a panther, and by an occultist group. We've had no time to think." She looked at Luke. "My friend needs a space to try and decipher the language. And I need a quiet space to journey. I need answers," Amelia said.

"Journey?" Luke asked.

"To the other side, dear," Hannah said. "To the spirit

world." She looked at Amelia with pride. "You do know that this woman is one of the most powerful magicians in London."

Luke raised his eyebrows as he glanced at Amelia.

"Hannah?" Amelia said, feeling uncomfortable about being given such a description. She doubted that it was true.

"Well, you are," Hannah said. "I'm a tarot reader and a witch, but I've never met anyone who can do half the stuff you can."

"Will you astral project?" Acacia asked. Her eyes brightened in anticipation.

"Yes, but I must sleep first," Amelia said. She needed to rest before she could focus her mind on astral travel.

Amelia felt her eyes closing as she lay down on the bed Acacia had kindly given her. Luke would sleep on the settee in the living room—if Rob and Dell ever stopped asking him questions. Whatever anybody might say about her friends, they were warm-hearted and loyal. If they were discovered, it wouldn't be because of anyone living here.

Amelia soon fell into a deep sleep, but several hours later she awoke inside a lucid dream. It was time to speak to her guides again, and this time away from distractions. Again, she was in a desert, and slowly the figures appeared before her. Victoria and Ernest were dressed in magician's robes, but Viktor and Teal had taken on a more martial appearance. Yet again, she had the feeling of being summoned to an exotic medieval court. The new leader of her guides, Viktor, sat in the centre of the semicircle. His metal armour shone with black light, and he carried a dark radiant sword.

*"You must prepare to fight,"* he said. His voice vibrated with martial energy, and the feeling was ominous, but his strength added to her confidence.

*"The last time we spoke you said that there were two things you had to tell me,"* Amelia said. *"First, that they would try to kill me. What was the second?"*

*"That help is available,"* he said. *"You must seek it."* His manner was terse, and he lapsed into silence.

*"What sort of help?"* They were silent, and she wondered whether they'd answer her question. *"How can I recognise this help?"*

Teal, a young athletic woman dressed in red-and-brown leather armour, left her throne and walked towards her. Teal usually appeared this way, and she usually wore a sword. It worried her that they now thought she needed two warriors to help her.

*"Look,"* Teal said, raising her hand. A vision appeared before her.

Fire raged all around, and Amelia gasped as the burning head of a woman looked at her. She recognised her from her vision. It wasn't normal fire but intense energy radiating from the woman. Her eyes glowed like burning embers, and her orange hair shone brightly.

*"What am I seeing?"* Amelia asked nervously. Her fear made the message harder to hear.

*"Some call her the Orange Witch,"* Teal said. The message was becoming unclear. *"Find her!"*

*"How?"* Amelia felt panicked as her guides faded from their desert thrones and their words became unclear. Teal spoke a final time, but her voice was fading fast. And then she was gone.

Amelia was alone with Viktor. *"Your enemy is her enemy. Summon her!"*

Amelia woke up shivering, despite the duvet. That was the most intense meeting she'd ever had with her guides. Normally, they just had a friendly chat. What disturbed her most was that her normally calm guides appeared nervous. She looked at the window. The curtain was drawn, but she could see the dawn light. Still some time. She settled back in the warmth of the bed again; she had to make one more journey.

She'd always considered herself to be a down-to-earth woman. She loved rally driving and never felt afraid racing her car along snowy forest tracks, but the vision of the witch with burning eyes scared her—there was something otherworldly about her. And although the message had been clear, she wanted to know more before attempting to directly summon the witch. Lying back in the bed, she closed her eyes, trying to calm herself, and eventually she felt relaxed enough to step outside her body and journey to another plane.

Aware that her body still rested in the bed, Amelia walked along the path she'd trodden many times before. This plane of existence could be tricky as it changed its appearance each time she entered it, but she recognised the path despite the changes in its outer appearance. Then, as if it had given up in its attempts to trick her, the path became familiar again.

*"I wish to visit the Akashic Records."*

Her intention took her to a dark forest, and she looked around, feeling a little disturbed. She wondered whether her fear had led her astray, but as she walked through the trees, a dark castle loomed through the mist. She walked towards it, wondering how to enter. She'd entered the Akashic Library before, but each time her point of entry had been different.

Nervous, but not wishing to appear so, she kept a steady pace. Aware that malevolent entities haunted these places, and that they could lead travellers to their deaths, she focussed on her task. The atmosphere was oppressive and seemed to be closing in on her. Seeing a stick, she picked it up and used it to force aside a branch. As she ducked underneath, it whipped back over her head.

She kept walking towards the castle, but as she walked, she felt a negative energy. It was getting closer. While demons inhabited this realm, it was possible that the energy emanated from the enemy. Death was no less likely on other planes of existence than it was on the material plane, and just because this world had a dreamlike quality didn't make it any less deadly. She had no wish for Acacia to find her dead body in her bed later in the day, and she walked faster, whilst still trying to move silently.

She was usually confident dealing with the dangers of this plane and had had a number of astral fights, but the mood of her guides had unsettled her, and the image of the witch had not comforted her at all. It seemed that, at best, the witch was the lesser of two evils. Fighting fire with fire.

A bird in the forest screeched. She stopped, searching for whatever had disturbed it. Something moved through the trees. She gasped as a black-robed figure sailed towards her, his robe billowing in some unfelt wind. He spoke the language of the killers. A dark vapour poured from his robe. She knew she mustn't touch it.

Her fear held her in place; it was a tactic some low-energy beings used. She had to lighten herself but wasn't sure how. It radiated fear and possibly fed on it, too. She felt the presence of her warrior guides. Viktor, with his dark, glowing sword, and Teal in her red-and-brown armour. They couldn't fight for her, but just the feeling of their presence gave her confidence.

Amelia imagined her stick was a blazing sword, and it appeared in her hand. The dark figure screeched and then attacked. She parried its blows, and it seemed surprised by her resistance. Then it disappeared into the forest. It was gone, which was often the way when facing evil. Simply fighting back was often enough to deter it. But not always.

Turning back toward the castle, she was surprised to find it directly in front of her. Amelia stood before an oak door and knocked.

*"I seek knowledge."*

The door swung open.

## 14

A multitude of galleries stretched into eternity. These were the memories of the universe. Searching for the tiniest fragments of information could take several lifetimes, unless you knew how. Amelia doubted that anyone ever came here to browse.

*"I seek the Orange Witch."*

The scene changed, and she found herself standing in a distant gallery. Amelia remembered the burning image of the witch, and an image of a forested world formed in front of her—a planet of ice and fire. She gasped, crying out. Something pulled her towards the planet.

*"Summon me."*

Amelia saw the witch in orange flames.

*"Open the path to your world."*

Amelia felt as if she were falling into darkness.

"It's alright," Hannah said.

She sat up in bed drenched in sweat and rubbed her eyes. "What time is it?"

"Just after six," Acacia said. "I'm normally still asleep now, but you woke me up."

"I'm sorry."

"No." Acacia shook her head. "This is serious."

Amelia remembered her journey. She was stiff and felt bruised, too, which sometimes happened after astral fights. Hannah and Acacia stood near to her, and slowly she calmed down.

"I was in the Akashic Library; you pulled me out."

"I'm sorry—"

Amelia interrupted her friend. "No. Something was pulling me towards it. And it's not alright."

The witch's message had been clear but unwelcome. Amelia had no idea what she'd be unleashing if she listened to the witch. If it hadn't been for the messages from her guides, she would certainly have ignored the woman. It was as if she'd found the telephone number of the witch in the library, called, and then connected with a presence living on an alien world. She shuddered, but despite her uncertainty, she knew what she was going to do.

"I have to perform a summoning."

"Amelia?" Hannah said. She saw concern in her eyes, although Acacia appeared merely curious.

"I don't have to perform it here, but I must call her."

"Who?" Acacia asked. "Who do you have to call?"

"The Orange Witch."

As she got dressed, she described her lucid dream, her visit to the Akashic Library, and the force that had pulled her to another place.

Both Hannah and Acacia went very quiet, which was unusual. But eventually, Hannah spoke. "So it's serious."

"It is."

They went downstairs. Luke lay on the settee.

"Luke?"

He slowly sat up and looked at his watch.

"Something's happened. I need to perform a summoning."

"What?"

She wasn't surprised he didn't understand. "I'm sorry to wake you."

"I wasn't really sleeping," he said.

"We're going to summon a witch," Acacia said.

Luke nodded but looked nonplussed.

With Hannah and Acacia's help, she rearranged the furniture to create a space in the centre of the living room. Amelia was relieved that Dell and Rob were still in bed. She liked them, but she wasn't sure she wanted to share this experience with any more people than necessary. Luke sat by the table and turned on the audio of the language. Amelia recognised it immediately from her dreams.

"I heard that language last night. The thing in the forest spoke it."

He stared at her without understanding. She realised that it was too early in the morning for either of them.

"I need you to turn the audio off."

He switched it off. "I'm getting there slowly. The device has speeded things up." From his expression, she guessed he was stuck. "I really need some sort of key."

She nodded. She was happy he was there. Both he and Hannah were fairly down to earth, unlike the very suggestible Acacia, whom she loved, but who sometimes became too excitable when anything psychic or occult was mentioned.

Amelia prepared a simple magic circle, partly for her own confidence, which was everything in a summoning. Although she'd witnessed two summonings, this was the first time she'd attempted one herself. She wished she had some of the initiates of her old order there. But her three friends were better than no one.

She also wished she knew more about controlling the entities that could appear when summoned. Low-energy entities sometimes appeared, hoping to feed on the summoner's vital energy. But she reminded herself that it wasn't a demon she was calling. If the witch turned out to be a demon, then she'd have a serious problem. But surely her spirit guides would never put her in that sort of danger. Then she thought of her new guide, the dark warrior, and she shivered.

Luke watched with a concerned expression. She guessed he was wondering what he'd got himself into, but she felt relief at having a non-believer present, which was the opposite of what she'd usually feel. In fact, this was the first time a complete outsider had observed her, but he was part of what was happening, and today she wanted a fully grounded observer.

She knelt on the outer edge of the circle with Hannah and Acacia sitting on either side. Luke watched them with an incredulous stare.

"What now?" Acacia asked.

"I'll call the witch. Once I begin, no one is to speak unless something happens."

"Happens?" Acacia repeated. Her brow wrinkled with concern.

"Nothing will happen," Hannah said. She smiled confidently.

"I need quiet," Amelia said.

The room went quiet, and she focussed on the image of the witch her guides had shown her, and the feelings she'd had when she'd been pulled to that distant place. Several minutes passed, and she breathed more deeply.

"I summon the Orange Witch."

She felt herself shifting towards another plane. The colours changed, and she left the room in London behind.

*"I call the Orange Witch."*

The image of the planet of ice and fire returned, and then she was in a steaming jungle. A pair of bright eyes watched her. She shuddered but focussed on her breathing. This was too real. A head materialised before her—the witch. She had bright orange hair, and her eyes were like burning embers.

*"Who are you?"* The woman's voice vibrated with power.

Amelia gasped, trembling involuntarily. *"Amelia Blake."*

*"Where?"*

*"In London."*

Amelia was now breathing heavily, but as she'd come this far, she was determined to push through her fear and ask her questions. She'd assumed the witch was human, but her energy felt different, and she was no longer so sure what it was she was speaking to. Fire bubbled from the witch's mouth, and Amelia's anxiety only increased as the figure burnt brighter in her mind. The fire was starting to hurt her.

*"I sense the enemy, but I need to know more."*

Amelia described the murders.

*"Green light?"*

*"It was described to me."*

*"Have you seen the killers?"*

Amelia shared an image of the man who hunted her. The witch watched, but then something happened. Her vision blurred, and she felt unsteady on her feet. Amelia gasped; she was now sweating heavily.

*"I must see more. Show me!"*

*"All right."*

Amelia was wondering what she'd just agreed to when

her memories flashed before her unbidden, but then stopped. A glimmering panther burnt in her mind.

*"How many of these have you seen?"*

*"Only the one."*

The witch paused. *"Anything else?"*

She shook her head.

*"Pray that's all there is because there's worse. The panther is a hunter—they have warriors, too."*

Amelia wasn't sure what she was talking about.

*"You spoke of a strange language. The text is familiar, but . . ."* The witch's voice faded. Then it was loud in her mind. *"Speak the language."*

*"I can't—"*

*"Speak!"* the witch commanded.

Images rushed through Amelia's mind—then they stopped. And she was reliving the moments before she'd entered the Akashic Library. The strange chanting figure in the billowing robes floated before her, and she shivered as the toxic cloud swirled around it.

*"You have a problem."*

The image vanished, and Amelia gasped. She mentioned the orange snow and the sickness.

*"Did they cause these things?"*

*"Perhaps."*

*"Where are they?"* Amelia asked. *"We need to know where to find them."*

She waited, and after several seconds she wondered whether the witch had left her. But then, more images flashed in her mind. Houses, faces, and things she didn't recognise, but then she heard trains passing behind her. In the distance was the familiar silhouette of Battersea Power Station.

Again, the witch moved through her memories, and an

image of Luke sitting, listening to the audio recording, appeared. The sounds of the alien language again played in her mind.

*"Have you heard the complete recording?"*

*"No."*

*"I must hear it."*

Amelia jerked upright, and Hannah and Acacia fell backwards and then crawled quickly away. She realised that she was sitting in the centre of the broken magic circle. Luke stared at her with bulging eyes. She wanted to tell her friends it was okay, but she could no longer speak. The witch spoke through her.

"Play!" she rasped in a strange voice.

Luke almost fell from his chair when his device played by itself.

"Write!" She spoke in this strange voice, but when Luke failed to move, she pointed at him and a pen rolled across the table. Luke grabbed it.

Amelia knew she was speaking, but she understood little of what she was saying. She was breathing heavily and felt nauseous, but she could see Luke scribbling into his notebook. And then she was finished.

Amelia struggled to think. She knew she had important questions to ask. *"What should we do?"* She found it an effort to even think.

"Kill them!" the witch said aloud through her. "No exceptions!" She vaguely sensed her friends looking at her in horror.

*"We can't just kill them; it's against—"*

*"There are no rules. Kill them!"*

Amelia felt as if she were about to burst into flames as she watched her friends edging towards the door. She heard herself speaking but wasn't aware of what she said. They stared wide-eyed at her.

"*Can you help?*" Amelia asked.

She immediately regretted her question. This apparition scared her, and she wondered why her guides had ever suggested making contact. For the first time in her life, she questioned their intentions. The witch grinned, and her fiery hair flickered around her head.

"*Perhaps.*"

"*What did you do?*" Amelia asked. She shuddered, sincerely wishing she'd never asked for help.

"*I planted a seed in your mind.*"

Amelia could no longer see the living room in London; the fiery figure occupied all her vision.

"*If a sorcerer attempts to kill you, call me.*"

"*How will I know what to say?*"

"*You'll know.*"

Amelia was now shivering uncontrollably. She felt as if a part of her mind had been parcelled off.

"*It was necessary,*" the witch said.

"*What will happen if I call you?*"

"*I'll use your body as a conduit; I'll come to you, wherever you are. I'll kill.*"

Amelia shuddered. "*What about me?*"

The witch was silent for several seconds before answering. "*If they become aware of my presence, they'll kill you.*"

Amelia's feeling of terror increased.

"*Speed will be vital.*"

The terrible burning head vanished, and Amelia opened her eyes. She was lying on the carpet staring at the peeling paper on the living room ceiling. She heard the door open and heard Hannah's voice.

"Luv, are you alright?"

Amelia tried to speak but couldn't. She let Hannah help her onto the sofa, and she sipped the cup of tea Acacia gave her. The carpet where she'd been lying was singed in the shape of her body. And there was a faint smell of burning.

She knew that nothing was alright.

## 15

Luke didn't believe in astral planes, telekinesis, or summonings, but he couldn't deny that something outside his experience had happened. The pen had rolled towards him, and the audio had played by itself. He thought it through several times and was certain he hadn't caused any of this. And then there was the translation Amelia had given him in the strange voice. Time would tell whether it made sense or not. Staring at the singed shape of a body on the carpet, he sipped his tea. Amelia sat on the sofa, and Acacia passed her another cup.

"It's alright now," Hannah said.

Luke hated trite comments. "She doesn't look alright."

Hannah and Acacia glared at him, but Amelia looked up. She seemed to be recovering. "No, it's okay." She rubbed her face with her hands.

"What happened?" Hannah asked.

"You heard some of it, and some parts I couldn't hear—when the witch translated."

"It's incredible," Luke said. "At least some of it seems to

make sense. I need more time." He looked down at the notes he'd scribbled in his notebook. "You said you heard trains."

"Yes, it was somewhere near Clapham Junction," Amelia said.

"Something was happening when you weren't speaking," Acacia said.

"The witch said things to me."

Luke found himself listening as intently as Hannah and Acacia.

"She was interested in the panther."

"What did she say about it?" Luke asked. He'd decided to suspend his disbelief for now. Anything that could help him find Molly was good.

"She said it's a hunter, but she said there were other things, warriors. And she told me to kill the men pursuing us."

"We heard that," Hannah said. "I hope you don't—"

"No, of course not," Amelia interrupted. "The witch spoke through me, but she doesn't control me."

"Can we trust what she said?" Hannah asked.

"I don't know. All I know is that she scared me."

"She scared the hell out of me, too," Hannah said. "Especially when you sat up and spoke in that strange voice."

Luke privately admitted to being very disturbed by all of this, too.

"I'm sorry about your carpet," Amelia said.

"It's old," Hannah said. "And it'll give us something to talk about."

Amelia's eyes lingered on the burnt spot, and Luke noticed her expression change. She was clearly frightened.

"Amelia? What's wrong?" Acacia asked, reaching out and holding her hand.

"She said something very dark."

Hannah squeezed up closer to her. "Amelia, you don't have to talk about any of this if you don't want to."

"She said she planted something inside me."

"Oh, don't listen to anything like that," Hannah said. "I don't want to say it's just your imagination, but it is possible to imagine some things even when others are accurate."

This was so strange for Luke. He was lost for words, but he just couldn't join in with this conversation. He heard Hannah and Acacia comforting her, but he was thinking about the house that may be near Clapham Junction Station and the van with Molly inside. It had disappeared in that direction. He was prepared to go from house to house until he found the grey van, and he'd start near the railway tracks.

For the first time since Molly had been taken, he felt his hope rekindled.

"Luke?" Amelia said.

"Sorry, I was thinking about Molly." They looked at him sympathetically. "The killer was driving the van towards Battersea last night. Molly might still be there. It's not that long ago; I have to find out."

"Shouldn't we plan something?" Amelia asked.

"I'm not sure there's much to plan. I'll walk from house to house until I find the van. I'll make a plan then." He had an urge to leave immediately. "I'm going alone. If anything happens to me, tell the police what's happened."

"No offence," Hannah said. "I mean, I'm not a fan of the police or anything, but shouldn't you just tell them, and then they can do this? It might be dangerous."

"No." He spoke at the same time as Amelia.

He reconsidered Amelia. Perhaps he should take her, but if things went wrong, he didn't want to risk her life.

"Rob might be able to help," Acacia said. "I can wake him up." She disappeared upstairs before Luke could say anything.

He shook his head. "I don't see how he could help."

"He used to be a thief," Hannah said.

Luke hesitated. A thief, even an ex one, might be useful. He nodded. "I'll wait."

As he waited, Luke suspected that he'd grown up more sheltered than he'd thought. These people belonged to a different world from the one he inhabited. Despite their oddness, he was beginning to like the inhabitants of the house, even if one was an ex-thief.

It wasn't long before Rob appeared. Luke waited while Hannah and Acacia gave a fragmented account of what had just happened. Rob stared at the singed carpet in amazement, then looked up at Luke.

"I don't thieve anymore," Rob said. Then he grinned. "But as they've kidnapped your wife, I'll break my personal rule."

"Thank you," Luke said.

"We can start near the tracks," Rob said.

"You're not thinking of trying to get inside, are you?" Hannah asked.

Luke knew his determination was drowning out what little sense of caution he felt. "I'll do anything I have to do to find my wife."

Acacia nodded. He sensed her approval.

"We need to learn all we can about these people," Amelia said.

"It's still early," Rob said. "They'll probably be sleeping now."

Luke raised his eyebrow. "How can you know that?"

"Thieves sleep in the morning," Rob said.

It made sense. It was just after seven o'clock, but despite getting hardly any sleep, Luke was ready to go. Then Acacia turned on the TV.

The news focussed on the murder, the orange snow falling in south London and Cheshire. And the strange sickness in the same areas. Scientists hoped to find a cure, but at least it wasn't fatal. There was speculation that the orange snow and sickness were connected, but no official confirmation had been given. When an expert suggested Russian involvement, Luke looked at his watch. It was already almost a quarter past seven. But the next piece of news caught his attention. "Five women have mysteriously disappeared in south London over the past week." Then the story changed.

"We need to go." He wanted to arrive before they could move Molly again.

Several minutes later, Luke, Amelia, and Rob were walking towards Clapham Junction. Both Luke and Amelia wore borrowed scarfs and woollen hats, partly for the cold and partly for disguise. They also wore backpacks. Luke had the translation device inside his. If Molly wasn't there, he'd collect all the evidence he could from the house.

When a police car passed, Rob laughed and pointed at some imaginary thing further down the street, distracting the police for a few seconds. They drove on. Clapham Junction was only a short walk, but despite the name, it wasn't in Clapham but in Battersea.

"I hope the panther isn't there," Amelia said.

"If the thing you've described is anywhere near, I'm calling this off," Rob said.

Luke silently agreed. He'd decided that if it was, he might call the police despite everything he'd said. Rescuing Molly was the most important thing, and if the police captured the real criminals, then he expected to be proven innocent.

"The witch said there were other things apart from the panthers," Amelia said.

"Do you believe her?" Luke asked. The shock he'd felt was wearing off.

She hesitated as they crossed a road, then seemed to decide. "I don't see why she'd make it up."

The only problem for Luke was that whatever facet of Amelia's imagination the witch represented, she wasn't real. Although, that didn't mean what she'd said wasn't true. Amelia might be intuitively interpreting information she'd been exposed to earlier. Things he'd missed. The influence of the unconscious was stronger than most people realised, and sometimes its contents spilt into consciousness. This wasn't the dominant view in modern psychology. Certainly not in cognitive psychology. Jung had been no more than a footnote when he'd been a student at university, and Luke had only read a little, but perhaps he should read more; his ideas might throw more light on Amelia's visions.

The thing he couldn't get out of his mind was how the audio recording had played by itself. Psychology didn't help him with that. Perhaps the shock of what was happening to Amelia had made him unconsciously click Play.

"Did she say any more?"

"Only what I've already told you about the hunters and the warriors."

Calling it a hunter made sense. It'd tracked them successfully so far. Although he knew it wasn't supernatural. Anything that could cut and burn like that was real, but it obviously came from somewhere.

He shivered, pulling his scarf tighter around his neck. The cold morning air was chilling.

"Do you think the panther could be part of a secret breeding programme?"

"Perhaps," Amelia said.

He was surprised she accepted the possibility so quickly.

She glanced at him. "The witch has supernatural powers, but that doesn't mean everything does."

He had no better theory to offer at the moment. If the criminals were arrested, then he was confident that the inexplicable would become explicable.

A train rattled past them towards Clapham Junction railway station. Luke had passed through it but never been there. He'd once read that it was the busiest station in Europe by the number of trains that passed through.

When Luke looked at the rows of houses, his heart sank. Despite his determination, he knew this could take a long time. By the fourth hour of the search, he was losing hope. Then Amelia spotted a grey van.

"Is that it?"

Luke regretted not taking the registration number, but it had been hard to see in the dim light. "It might be. It's the same make."

It was parked in front of a row of terraced houses next to the railway tracks.

"I know these houses," Rob said. "I tried to rob them years ago, but a dog disturbed me."

"But which house?" Luke asked. He realised they couldn't just knock on the doors.

"It would be easier to enter from the rear," Rob said.

He led them down a path, then turned left towards the tracks. They were at the back of the houses. Each had a long wooded garden that adjoined the railway tracks.

"This way."

He climbed over a fence, and soon they found themselves walking through the rear of someone's garden. They climbed another fence into the second garden and stopped.

"Why here?" Luke asked. There were several more houses further on.

"We can watch the first three houses from here," Rob said. "As soon as we eliminate one, we can move on."

"This could take hours," Luke said.

"Days," Rob replied.

The first house had children's toys spread over the snow-covered lawn, and like the first, the one in front of them had a well-kept garden. He looked through the trees at the back of a pale blue terraced house to the right. Someone had tended the garden, but it had a bleaker feel.

"They don't use the garden," Rob said. He'd seen Luke looking. "But that doesn't mean much really. We just have to wait."

"What's that?" Amelia asked. She pointed to the far side of the lawn behind the pale blue house.

"What?" Luke couldn't see anything.

Rob shrugged. "Something's disturbed the snow."

"I think we should check," Amelia said.

"I'll take a look," Rob said. He hopped over the fence and moved quickly through the bushes at the end of the garden. Several seconds later, he returned. "Come."

Rob was gone again before Luke could question him, and he followed Amelia over the fence. As soon as Luke saw the large animal prints on the lawn, he knew it was the panther. Nothing else could make such large prints, not unless a tiger had escaped from a nearby zoo.

Amelia looked at the blue house through the bushes. "I don't want to go in if that thing's here."

Luke strained to see the nearest prints without falling out of the bushes. "I don't think it is."

Amelia raised an eyebrow.

"He's right," Rob said. "The tracks move away from the house. They were only made a few hours ago."

"Are you a tracker?" Amelia asked.

"No, but I know some things. They're not fresh; they've started to fill with snow again."

They followed the path the tracks took through the trees to the fence dividing the house from the railway tracks. After waiting for another train to pass, Rob climbed over.

"The snow's a deeper shade of orange here," Amelia said quietly as they watched Rob.

Luke had noticed it, too. "I wonder if there's sickness in the area." He felt a little queasy, but he'd put it down to nerves.

A few yards from the fence, Rob knelt. "It jumped over. There's a deeper impression here." He pointed down the tracks. "It went that way."

"Now we just have to break in," Luke said. He was surprised at his nerves—he'd thought his anger would have overridden every other feeling, but he was wrong. He stepped forward but felt a hand on his shoulder.

"Not so fast," Rob said. "We wait."

"What for?" Luke saw no point in delaying this. He could see that no one was in the kitchen extension.

Rob took out a small pair of binoculars. "I want to see if anyone's inside the living room."

"The curtains are closed," Luke said.

"Not perfectly closed. There's a gap," Rob said.

Luke was irritated by the wait. He glanced around the garden for a possible weapon, wishing he'd thought about this before, but he realised that perhaps there was no point. He had no idea how to use a weapon. For the first time in his life, he regretted his peaceful boyhood. He'd only been in one fight at school, and that had been more of a scuffle.

"There's no movement. Let's go," Rob said.

The ex-thief led the way through the snow directly towards the sliding glass doors.

## 16

"Have you ever broken into a house?" Rob asked as he looked through a narrow gap between the curtains.

"Only with a brick," Luke said.

Rob grinned. "I'll show you how the experts do it. And in under three seconds."

Luke didn't believe him; he was bragging.

Rob grinned at his expression. "Time me."

He positioned a screwdriver under the door and pushed down on it, raising the door slightly. He then pulled on the handle, and it opened.

Luke's eyes widened in surprise.

"These are the easiest, but french windows aren't much harder."

If he lived through this, Luke promised himself that he'd review his home security, before remembering the fire that had destroyed most of his house.

They walked inside. The room was half library and half workshop. Bookshelves lined the walls, but a table in the centre dominated the room. A large device that looked like a miniature version of Battersea Power Station, but with an extra chimney in the centre that glowed red, sat on the table. It made a faint humming sound.

"What is it?" Amelia asked.

Luke shook his head. He had no idea. Orange dust covered the carpet. He took some photos. Then, moving to the door, he listened, but the house was silent.

"I want to search the house," Luke said.

Amelia looked at him from one of the bookshelves. She nodded, continuing to look through the books. Opening the door, Luke looked into the dark hallway and waited. Still hearing no sound, he walked down the hallway and stopped at what he assumed was the living room door. He opened it slowly. The room was dark and empty; there was no sign it was being used. Next, he went into the kitchen; Rob checked the downstairs toilet. All were empty.

A sound came from upstairs, and Luke and Rob quickly rejoined Amelia. Footsteps came down the stairs. Two men, and by their accents, it was clear that they were locals. Rob hid behind the door, and Luke and Amelia stood behind the curtains, but the footsteps went into the kitchen. The men opened a cupboard, and a few minutes later Luke smelt cheap coffee. Someone opened a plastic bag.

"When's the weirdo coming?" one of them asked.

"Which one? The angel of death or his master?"

"The foreign git," the first man said.

"I don't know, but Angel's coming here this morning."

The first man cursed. "I'll kill him after we've finished this job."

"He's ex-special forces. He'd do you in without a blink."

"I'll wait till he's high," the first man said. "It's Olney that's dangerous."

They turned the radio on.

Luke guessed that the man who'd kidnapped his wife

was Angel. He wasn't certain who Olney was; perhaps he'd been one of the men in hoods chanting over Leander Amis's body.

"I need to look upstairs," Luke whispered.

Rob rested his hand on Luke's shoulder. "It's safer if I go. I know how to be quiet. Take what you want from here, but be ready to leave fast." Before Luke could say anything, he'd opened the door, slipped out, and was creeping up the stairs.

"Let him do what he can do best," Amelia whispered. "We need to learn more about these people." She pointed to the shelves and drawers.

Luke nodded, and they searched the room. He looked for documents, photographs, or anything that might give more information on the kidnappers. He stopped in front of a large painting of an alien landscape. A dried-up riverbed wound through a futuristic-looking city. He studied the bends in the river.

"That looks like the Thames," he said. "But the sun's brighter."

Amelia stared at the painting; her mouth fell open.

"What?" he asked.

"That's one of the images I've seen in my visions and dreams."

She appeared shocked. He made a decision to take her dreams and visions seriously, especially after the strangeness of what had happened in her friends' house.

"My guides told me that these people are not from our world," she said.

The idea was odd. He stood back and took a picture of the painting with his phone. Then he returned to the books lining the shelves. Many were bound in leather and smelt old. Surely aliens wouldn't use physical books. But he realised he couldn't know that. What if they just liked them? He opened one, and the script was similar to the text he'd already seen. He picked out another, but the text was impossible to read.

"Search for any with pictures or diagrams," he said.

Amelia was already helping herself to many of the books, and he did the same. Then he noticed a well-worn notebook stuffed behind a book. Flicking through it, he smiled.

"What?" Amelia whispered.

"Someone's been studying English at a local college." He added it to his growing collection. His backpack was already getting heavy; he'd have to be more selective about what else he took. But he was pleased with the notebook. With Amelia's partial translation, it could be the key to learning the language.

The door opened, and his heart leapt.

"You look like you've seen a ghost," Rob said. Before Luke could speak, he continued. "There's nothing upstairs, but people have been sleeping rough in one of the rooms."

"It could be the criminals," Luke said, gesturing towards the kitchen.

Rob shook his head and held up a pair of leggings. "I found these, too. Are they your wife's?"

They weren't, but Luke took them anyway. They could be evidence for the police in the future.

"One more thing," Rob said. "There's a padlock on the outside of the door."

"How many people slept there?" Amelia asked.

Rob shrugged. "Hard to say. There're three mattresses on the floor. The room's dirty."

"I want to listen to more of what they're saying," Luke said.

Rob moved back to the sliding glass windows and carefully pulled aside the curtains to watch the kitchen.

Luke's backpack was heavy enough, and he took out his device and put it to the door. It could record as well as translate. The first man was loud and repugnant. He bragged about raping a woman. Luke chilled. If it was Molly . . . He seldom had violent thoughts, but now they turned to murder.

The back door slammed.

"Two men," Rob whispered.

"Angel," the first man said. His voice quavered.

"I heard you," Angel said. "You should have shut the window."

"I was just playing."

"I told you not to touch them."

The kitchen was otherwise silent.

"I'll pay." The man's voice became shrill.

A piece of crockery fell to the floor. Rob was frantically whispering something, but Luke continued listening by the door, hoping to hear something of Molly. He heard a gasp, and something heavy fell to the floor.

"You've killed him," the second man said. There was fear in his voice.

"I'll kill anyone who touches them." No one spoke. "Has anyone been in the back room?"

"No," the second man said.

As Luke stared at the softly humming device on the table, he prayed for Molly.

"We may have to run," Rob said.

Luke nodded. He tried to calm down. Helping Molly required a cool head; he was worried he was becoming too nervous.

"Look," Amelia whispered. She pointed into an open drawer. Inside was an ornate knife.

"The murder weapon," he whispered. One of the men kneeling next to Leander Amis had held it.

"Don't touch it," she said. "It's our evidence."

He found a piece of cloth, wrapped it around the handle, and put it in his coat pocket. Amelia added some more books to her bag, including the large one with drawings.

Rob was still looking through the window.

"I want to leave," Luke said. He was scared of the killers. Especially Angel. And he wasn't sure he could outrun them, not if his backpack got any heavier. He put down a book he was holding.

Rob nodded. "We may have to sprint."

"They look fit," Amelia said.

That's what Luke feared. "They're leaving the kitchen. Let's go."

He took a final photograph of the strange glowing device on the table. Just being close to it made the hairs on his arms stand up.

Rob cursed.

Something was pressing against the outside of the curtains.

"Get away from the window," Luke whispered as he moved quickly behind the door.

The panther pushed through the curtains; its head was inches from Rob.

"Back away!" Luke said.

Amelia was already moving when the panther's mouth opened, and fire burnt Rob's shoulder. He cried out as he fell to the floor. The panther stepped over him, more interested in Amelia. She rushed towards Luke, knocking into the humming device. Something changed, and all the hairs on Luke's body rose. The humming became louder, and all four chimneys glowed red.

"I didn't do anything," Amelia said.

Luke held the sacrificial knife in his hand, no longer caring about fingerprints. Amelia stood by his side, shaking as the panther forced them back against the wall. The sound of the device changed from a hum to a whine, the panther moaned and backed away, moving towards the window. Luke noticed that Rob had already crawled outside.

The door flew open, and Luke felt his legs weaken with fear. Angel strode into the room; Luke recognised him immediately. He didn't see Luke and Amelia standing in the shadows by the bookshelves. Luke watched the lean and wiry man from behind as he inspected the glowing device.

"Did you do this?" Angel said.

He seemed to be speaking to the panther, which was backing into the garden. It mewled and continued to back away. Then, turning, it ran through the garden, taking the fence at the end of the garden in a single leap. Rob sprinted after it.

Angel saw Rob and walked quickly towards the window. Luke and Amelia took advantage of the distraction and rushed through the open door into the hallway, but Luke hit a small table, dropping the translation device to the floor.

"Stop them!" Angel shouted.

Two men rushed out of the kitchen, but Luke was already opening the front door. He ran outside, and Amelia slammed the door shut after her, but it opened almost immediately. The bigger man pushed past his partner.

"I can handle them." It was the man who had entered with Angel. "Just a woman and some professor. You can stop that damn sound."

The other man protested, but the bigger one forced him back inside.

Luke and Amelia ran down the street in the direction of Battersea Fire Station, chased by the man.

"Faster!" Amelia said. She was pulling ahead of him. They'd almost reached the end of the street.

He was gasping for breath, and the man was getting closer. But an explosion threw them to the ground. He felt Amelia shaking him.

"Get up!"

"What happened?" he gasped, picking himself up.

"The house exploded." She pointed to where the thug lay on the ground. Behind him, a fire raged. It had already engulfed the houses on either side. "I did that." Her voice was flat.

"Are you okay?"

She nodded. "You?"

"Yes." He was only grazed. He picked up his dirty backpack.

People were rushing out of their houses, moving away from the flames.

"Look," Amelia said.

The man who had been chasing them stood and glared, and then he charged. Luke and Amelia turned left and ran past Battersea Fire Station, turning left again onto the main road leading to the tunnel. The man was not losing energy. He was gaining on them. No one seemed to notice the three people running down the road, not with the blazing fire and smoke pouring into the air from the row of houses. Fire engines were already leaving the station, their sirens adding to the feeling of chaos.

Luke's limbs slowed despite his efforts to keep moving. Amelia was struggling, too. He'd slowed to a jog, but at least he was moving, and soon they entered the tunnel under the railway tracks. A man approaching them from the opposite direction looked up, alarmed, and quickly crossed the road. Then Luke heard footsteps behind him. The criminal tackled him, and he went down under the heavy weight of the man's body. He lay on the ground grazed and winded. The man was already on his feet. He grabbed hold of Amelia, throwing her into the side of the tunnel.

"You're not going anywhere!" the man said. Amelia's head hit the wall of the tunnel, and Luke watched the man's hands tighten around her throat. He struggled to stand. His body hurt all over, and he felt lightheaded.

"Help!" she gasped.

"He won't help you," the man said. "He's not the sort; he'll watch me kill you, and then he'll let me kill him, too." He sneered at Luke.

Luke stood up, using the dirty tunnel wall for support. He was scared but also desperate. His single school scuffle hadn't equipped him for this; he didn't know what to do. The man smirked as he casually stared at Luke with one hand around Amelia's throat. Luke looked around, realising that they were alone in the tunnel. No one could help them.

"When I've killed you, I'll have fun with your wife, too." The man gave a short laugh and turned his attention back to Amelia.

Seeing Amelia gasping for breath and hearing the threat to Molly was too much. In anger, he reached inside his pocket and took out the ceremonial dagger. As he stepped closer, he noticed that Amelia's face was turning blue—she was dying. The man was paying no attention to him. Luke guessed he wasn't worthy of that.

Luke stabbed the man in his back, and as he turned, he stabbed him again. The man's eyes widened in surprise, and he staggered towards Luke. It was then that Luke lost control, stabbing him repeatedly, and when he fell, Luke followed him down, still stabbing.

"You can stop now, he's dead," Amelia said. "But you took your time." Amelia was gasping and rubbing her throat.

"I've never killed a man before," Luke said.

A woman screamed from the pavement on the opposite side of the tunnel. A car stopped next to her, and a man leant out of the open window and started videoing the scene.

Amelia took his hand. "We have to go." They turned and ran back towards Battersea.

"Murder!" the woman screamed.

## 17

Jack's skin smarted from the heat, even from thirty yards away. Flames had engulfed the row of houses, and although Battersea Fire Station was only a hundred yards away, the fire was already out of control.

Local residents were leaving their houses with their children and pets, directed by dozens of police. A line of ambulances waited, but the bodies lined along the pavement would have to wait until the injured were ferried to local hospitals.

Whoever had done this would pay.

He had no doubt his country was under attack from a foreign group, and that they were using locals to assist them. The UK threat level had been raised from substantial to severe, meaning that an attack was seen as highly likely, and MI5 was hunting the killers round the clock. The rest of Red Team were nearby, though not distinguishable from members of the public. The suspects had been seen running from the area seconds after the blast.

He answered his radio.

"Jack, we've found them." It was Alice, the team coordinator at Thames House.

"Where?" Jack was already heading towards the high street.

"They're walking down Prince of Wales Drive, next to Battersea Park. I want Red Team to move in. Randall will pick you up on the corner of Este Road."

"Roger that."

The Triumph Bonneville stopped at the corner of the street, and Jack mounted without speaking. Randall rode fast, running a red light and swinging right onto Battersea Park Road. Jack suspected that permission to ignore traffic regulations had been given. Randall took a sharp left, slowing as they approached Prince of Wales Drive. On the far side of the road was Battersea Park.

"They're there," Randall said.

Jack dismounted. He'd already seen them. They were about twenty yards to the left, on the other side of the road, walking by the park.

"Where are the others?" Jack asked.

"Bonnie and Pete are in position in the park. Steve's at Rosery Gate. Claire should be here soon." Randall left without further comment. Jack saw him stop further down the road, opposite Macduff Gate. Red Team were almost in position.

Jack stood on the corner with his phone in his hand, but his eyes were on the approaching suspects. He disliked the habit of stopping to stare into a screen in the middle of a street, but for an MI5 operative, it had advantages—there was nothing else to look at apart from bushy hedges and rows of Victorian houses.

He watched the suspects approach. For such regular-looking people, they'd left a horrific trail of destruction across London. But now the net was closing around them. About fifteen yards behind the suspects, a man in a black hoodie was walking his dog. Jack wondered about the breed. It was unusually large and was wearing the kind of dog costume that usually only lapdogs wore—a hideous black-and-purple cape with an attached hoodie obscuring its face. He shook his head in disgust. That was no way to treat an animal, but then his attention switched back to the suspects. They'd just entered Battersea Park.

He spoke to Thames House. "They've just passed through Alexandra Gate. I'm following them into the park."

"Roger that, Jack," Alice said. "Red Team's in position. Bonnie will take over if they turn to the north side of the lake."

"Where are the police?" Jack asked.

"In position on all corners of the park but are waiting for the Firearms Unit."

"How long?"

"Five minutes."

Jack let the suspects walk several yards into the park before walking to the zebra crossing opposite the gate. The hooded man with the dog followed them into the park. There was something familiar about him, but he couldn't place it. When the man wandered into the trees with his dog, Jack followed the suspects, who both wore backpacks.

The suspects turned right, towards the water. Two pieces of land jutted into the lake, coming together like a set of crab's claws. The claws were connected by a footbridge. The suspects walked towards one of the claws. On either side of them was water. He felt satisfied. They'd chosen the perfect position for the police to arrest them.

Alice spoke again. "Bonnie's got them now. You can drop back, Jack."

"Roger that."

When the suspects wiped the snow from a bench and sat down, Jack did the same, sitting on a bench about twenty yards away. Bonnie was taking photographs of the lake from the other side of the footbridge.

The suspects were between two pincers.

Now all they had to do was observe and wait for the Firearms Unit to get in position. Then the police would make the arrest. If he'd been a secret service operative in some countries, he'd have been issued with a gun and would've made the arrest himself. But in Britain it wasn't done that way. MI5 operatives were unarmed, as were the regular police.

He waited.

The Firearms Unit arrived, moving into position around him. One moved through the undergrowth opposite him, and a second moved into the bushes near Bonnie. A third was to the east of the lake, and the final one on the south side. Regular police units blocked the path to his right and the one behind Bonnie. Reserves waited at all four corners of the park. Jack suspected the suspects would surrender; they didn't look like the types to put up a fight, but looks could be deceptive. A man had been murdered near the scene of the explosion, and the suspect for that crime matched Dr Lee's description. It was almost certain they had knives, perhaps worse. If their backpacks contained bombs, it could get messy. Jack glanced at the police gathering to his right; they were just out of view of the suspects. They'd been told that MI5 was operating in the area.

"We've lost contact with Sergeant Higgs." One of the constables was speaking to the police sergeant.

Higgs was the police marksman on the east side of the lake. It was probably nothing, but he never, even when he was not on an operation, stopped searching his surroundings for possible threats. He watched the shores of the lake and the wooded islands carefully. The police sent someone to check. A minute later a call informed them that Higgs was missing. Suspecting the worst, Jack watched the suspects. They appeared oblivious to the net tightening around them. Between them, on the bench, was a growing pile of books, which occupied their attention completely. The police radio mentioned a van driving past the outdoor cafe. All driving inside the park was against regulations, and the park police were investigating. Two coincidences were too many.

He turned on the radio. "Bonnie, can you see anything?"

"All quiet here."

The sergeant decided to proceed with only three shooters in position. The nearest two covered all possibilities, the third was there in case anyone broke through the police lines, but Jack seriously doubted that they'd swim across the lake.

Taking a megaphone, the sergeant stood in the centre of the pathway.

"This is the police!"

The two suspects looked up, appearing startled.

"You're under arrest. Stand up slowly and put your hands in the air, and then walk towards us. Dr Lee first, followed by Ms Blake."

The suspects started to stuff things back into their backpacks.

"There are police marksmen on either side with orders to shoot if you make any sudden movements. Put the bags down and walk slowly towards me with your hands in the air."

A cry came from near the footbridge.

"Bonnie, what's happening?"

"Something's moving in the undergrowth."

Jack couldn't see clearly because of the trees.

Bonnie sprinted over the bridge towards the suspects. Behind her, a police shooter was shooting at something in the undergrowth.

"Bonnie, what's wrong?"

"An animal," she said. "It's got the firearms officer."

Jack had heard about police officers being cut to pieces on Clapham Common. The police marksman near Jack was already moving down the path towards the suspects, who stood with their hands in the air. Bonnie had reached the bench and was checking their bags, but she kept glancing back at the bushes on the far side of the bridge.

A shot rang out, and the police marksman near Jack fell to the ground. He was dead. Someone was in the trees behind Bonnie. The operation had gone badly wrong. A panther walked from the bushes on the other side of the bridge. It snarled as it crossed the bridge. It was bigger than it should have been, and its eyes glowed. It was more than strange that in one day he'd encountered two types of creatures that shouldn't exist. From the way the two suspects stood frozen, he was sure they hadn't expected any of this. He listened to the sergeant radio the final police marksman. He was already on his way, but it would take him three or four minutes to reach them.

Then Bonnie screamed.

Jack chilled as he watched the man in the black hoodie put a pistol to Bonnie's head. It was the man he'd seen walking the monstrosity of a dog, which he now realised had been the panther in disguise. Bonnie fought hard, but the man was strong and tightened his grip of her neck. Dr Lee appeared to remonstrate with him. The man pointed his pistol at Lee, but

Bonnie tried to take the gun. The man fired. Nothing about this was as Jack had expected. Dr Lee lay on the ground, bleeding from his head. Amelia Blake knelt next to him.

Jack was on the radio to Thames House. "Permission to arm myself."

"Jack?"

Bonnie elbowed the man in the stomach, and for a few seconds the man struggled before regaining control, but the scuffle caused his hood to fall down. Jack's eyes widened in recognition.

"He's dead!"

He'd forgotten he was still speaking to Alice.

"Keep your emotions under control! We need you to follow orders," Alice said.

"I know the killer."

Alice went quiet for a moment. "Who is it?"

"William Angel Provost. Thirty-eight years old." He knew she was typing the information into her computer. "Ex-SBS commando, court-martialled and jailed."

"For drug abuse—"

Jack interrupted. "That's only what they got him for."

"Did you serve with him?"

"Yes . . . He shot a family in the mountains. Executed unarmed prisoners, too."

"Why did he shoot the family?"

"He said they were aiding insurgents."

"Were they?"

"Probably. Many of the rebels came from those villages."

Angel dragged the struggling Bonnie towards the other suspects. He had a pistol to her head. Lee was lying on the ground and not moving; Blake was attempting to resuscitate him. She made no attempt to escape.

"Jack," Alice said. "I want you to wait for Pete and Randall. Randall has a gun license."

"I'm trained."

"He has a license, Jack."

Jack turned off the radio.

"Put the gun down and surrender," the police sergeant said.

Angel looked up, his eyes widening. "Sergeant Ross. What a surprise."

The police sergeant glanced at Jack.

"I presume the police sergeant doesn't know you, Jack."

Amelia Blake was still kneeling on the ground but was now staring at him.

"Let her go, Angel."

The man was on drugs. Jack shuddered; history was repeating itself.

Angel smirked. "You didn't call me that last time, Jack."

"She's done nothing," Jack said.

"She works for the Security Service," he barked.

He shot Bonnie in the head and dropped her body to the ground. A brutal execution. For nothing. He'd done this before; Jack had watched him. And now Bonnie lay motionless on the ground, blood flowing from her head.

If Jack had had a gun, he'd have shot Angel dead without hesitation, career be damned. But the nearest weapon lay next to the dead police marksman ten yards away. Although the members of Red Team never socialised and hardly ever spoke of personal matters, he did know Bonnie left behind a young child.

Angel grabbed Amelia Blake by the hair, dragging her towards the lake.

"You're surrounded," the sergeant said.

But Angel ignored the police. "I'm sure we'll meet again, Jack."

"You just killed a young mother," Jack shouted.

"She shouldn't be working for the Security Service."

Angel hissed, and the panther rushed at the police officers, sending them backwards. It slashed the leg of one who was too slow. Angel pulled Blake into the water. Like Bonnie, she struggled, but she wasn't as strong as Bonnie, and he controlled her more easily. With one arm around her throat, he swam across the channel to the island several yards away.

The panther prevented both Jack and the police from following or reaching the gun. It stared at him, its eyes glinting briefly. Then it was gone, diving into the water to follow its master. He didn't see it crawl ashore with Angel—the undergrowth was too thick—but he knew it was there from the sounds birds on the island raised. He also knew they wouldn't be on the small thickly wooded island long.

Jack ran past the police to where Bonnie lay. His heartbeat pounded. He was going to kill him. He'd had the chance once on a mountain path, after the operation, but he'd chosen to do the right thing and let the murderer live. And now Bonnie was dead. He'd had enough of doing the right thing. Jack walked over to the body of Lee. He was still breathing. When Jack touched him, he opened his eyes.

"The things in the bags." The man gasped for breath.

"That's none of your business now," an approaching police officer said.

But Jack listened. He was no longer so sure that this man, or the woman who'd been taken hostage, were as guilty as the police thought.

"We took from the house in Battersea. They may help identify the killers." The man's eyes were flickering. He was flushed and breathing heavily. "They had a device. Amelia knocked it by mistake, and it started to vibrate. I think it caused the explosion."

"You can leave him now," the sergeant said.

Jack wanted to pursue Angel, but he also needed to learn more.

Lee continued. "The man called Angel was in Leander Amis's house, and in the house in Battersea. He controls the panther."

"Is he the mastermind?" Jack asked.

"No, there's a man called Olney . . ." Lee gasped as a medic examined him. "A foreigner. Amelia thinks he's an alien."

"How is he?" Jack asked the medic. He wondered if the man was delirious.

"Not as bad as he looks. I don't know if was on purpose or whether the shooter was just a bad shot, but the bullet just grazed him. He'll be okay."

Jack knew Angel was one of the best shots. Bonnie had caused him to miss.

"Angel kidnapped my wife. He's evil."

"I know," Jack said.

Lee struggled to sit up, but the medic put a restraining hand on his chest. "Don't move," he said.

Lee collapsed back to the ground and looked up at Jack. "Help me find my wife!"

Jack gave a short nod, but his thoughts were soon interrupted by Pete and Randall.

"Provost's heading for Rosery Gate," Jack said. "Steve's there."

"How do you know where he's going?" Randall asked.

"A guess. It's the nearest gate from the other side of the island."

"We have orders to pursue," Pete said.

Both Pete and Randall began to run back along the path. Jack watched them and then looked at the island.

"Joining us?" Randall asked.

"I'll see you at Rosery Gate," Jack said.

He rushed into the water, wading and then swimming to the island. Someone shouted something about the panther, but Jack was already pushing into the undergrowth. He knew the animal was long gone. He moved quickly, ignoring scratches from the thick vegetation. A minute later he stood on the far side of the small island. The footprints in the mud showed him where Angel had dragged out the struggling woman. He waded straight into the water and then swam the short distance to the shore, wondering the fastest way to Rosery Gate. Automatic weapons fire guided him towards it. He sprinted past two young women and a dog walker who were moving quickly away from the trouble.

Jack prayed that it was the firearms officers shooting, but he knew Angel. He was more deadly than a dozen police officers. Jack only slowed when he came in sight of the gate. There was a grey van parked nearby. He couldn't see Blake; perhaps she was inside the van. Bodies lay on the path and around the entrance. He ran into the wooded area, hiding behind a tree and cursing his lack of a firearm.

The shooting stopped.

Angel stood next to a taller man, who Jack guessed was Olney. He was also wearing a black hood. Both held assault rifles. Steve lay dead on the ground, and the bodies of six or seven dead police officers lay near him. Jack was sickened. It'd been a massacre. These had been unarmed police; they hadn't stood a chance. The driver of the van stared open-mouthed at the bodies. Jack guessed the man was a local criminal, paid to do a job, and who was now in well over his head.

Without showing a single emotion, the two men climbed into the van. The terrified driver accelerated towards a remaining cluster of police officers, sending them scattering across the road.

## 18

Ruth walked down a carpeted passage deep underground in a section of Thames House she hadn't known existed an hour earlier. She was still tired after the night at Shakerley Manor; her hopes of taking a nap had gone. It was late on Saturday afternoon, and she was already behind schedule, having got lost in the labyrinth of passages, and was nervous at the prospect of the meeting some of the most powerful people in Britain.

Her phone vibrated as she approached the sound-proofed meeting room. If she'd already been inside the room, the call wouldn't have reached her.

"Jack?" She was irritated. They'd agreed not to speak until next week. "I'm late for a meeting."

"I need to talk to you—"

"Can't this wait?"

"Bonnie and Steve have been killed."

She stopped in the passage. "Are you alright?"

"I'm okay, but Bonnie was executed in front of me."

"Oh my God!" She'd never met his colleagues in Red Team, but she'd heard their names and knew they were close. She listened to what she guessed was the abbreviated version. "When did this happen?"

"This morning. I've already spoken to the police. I think the two suspects are innocent. I saw their reaction when Bonnie was murdered, and when they saw the killer."

"Who?"

"Angel Provost. We served together. I told you about him."

"I remember."

"He shot Dr Lee, too, but the bullet just grazed him. He's lucky to be alive. He was delirious, mentioning aliens or something, but the medic said he'd be okay. What I do know is that a foreign group is attacking our country." He paused. "I'll let you get to your meeting."

"I've found new things inside the snow," she said.

"Tell me later. But one more thing."

"What?"

"There was an animal with Angel."

"A panther?" She'd read the reports.

"Its eyes glowed."

Ruth almost laughed. "What?"

The man by the entrance of the meeting room coughed.

"Jack, I'm being called into the meeting."

She hung up and walked inside the plush meeting room. When she realised that she had been the last person to enter, she felt her cheeks burning in embarrassment, especially when she saw the new home secretary watching her from the head of the table.

"Good of you to join us, Ms Hardy," Robert Best, the head of MI5, said as she entered.

This was the first time since she'd joined MI5 that she'd been late for a meeting. It wasn't something she did. But here, in front of the most senior people in the country, she was late.

"I'm sorry. I had an important call . . ."

The men and women in the room all watched her.

"From . . ." She didn't want to say from her boyfriend. "From someone with information on the situation."

The head of MI5 nodded, and she took her seat next to Derek White, the head of the biological and chemical warfare unit. He'd been studying the chemical composition of the snow. There were seven people in the meeting, including herself, and she knew the names of all but two.

Rebecca Smith, the new home secretary, sat at the head of the table. To her left was Best; to her right was a man Ruth didn't recognise but suspected was the head of MI6. Then there was Gordon Wells, the deputy head of the Counter Terrorism Unit. The last person was a senior naval officer sitting to her right.

The home secretary spoke first.

"On the advice of both MI5 and MI6, we've increased the terror threat level in the UK from severe to critical. It seems another attack is highly likely." She glanced at the head of MI5.

Best nodded. "A foreign military team appears to be working in our country."

The naval officer was the only one who appeared surprised. "Which foreign power?"

"We suspect Russia," the head of MI6 said.

"Are you sure?" the admiral asked.

"No, but—"

"They're the likely suspects," Best said. "We suspect the language is an obscure Russian dialect."

Ruth knew that deciphering the language was proving almost impossible. It was also strange that almost everyone who had been working on the project was dead. They'd tried to kill Dr Lee, too. Like Jack, she wondered exactly what his involvement was. Whether he was involved in the murder or not, he appeared to be their best chance of understanding the language.

"According to Dr Lee, something catastrophic is going to happen at sunrise tomorrow. He claims that Leander Amis left him a letter expressing his concern. Unfortunately, we can't confirm this, but we have to take the threat seriously. It's already four o'clock, and we've got no idea what he was talking about. I hope someone has something new to tell me."

There was silence. And then the head of MI5 looked at Ruth. She felt like shrinking in her seat but instead forced herself to sit upright.

"I've found something new in the snow. Something that shouldn't be there."

Everyone listened carefully.

"First, I've continued to find the orange crustaceans—"

"It's strange that there are shrimps in the snow, but it hardly helps us determine what the problem is," the head of MI6 said.

"Crustacean shells in the coral sand," Ruth corrected.

"Get to the point," he said.

Trying not to feel flustered, Ruth continued. "The bodies of the crustaceans have been hard to identify, but there are similar sorts of coral sand in some parts of the world. What we found this morning is substantially different." Best leant forward, but before he could interrupt her, she quickly continued. "We've found a new species of crustacean; a kind of prawn."

The admiral raised his eyebrows, and the home secretary smiled.

"From the segments we've found, we estimate that it measures three feet long."

Now she had their complete attention.

"We believe it has eighty legs, as opposed to the more normal ten. And it has horns."

"Where does it come from?" Wells asked.

"This sample was found near the house that exploded in Battersea, but we've found something similar in Cheshire."

"Yes, but I mean where did it originally come from?"

"I've got no idea." The expressions around the table darkened. "I mean, there's nothing like this anywhere. It's like something from prehistoric times."

"You mean it's a dinosaur fragment?" Best asked.

Ruth regretted using the word prehistoric. "We've already checked, but I've not been able to find any records of prehistoric animals like this."

"But it's possible that the explosion has unearthed sets of prehistoric fossilised remains?" Wells said.

"Perhaps." Ruth really had no idea. "But it's strange that the same types of remains have been found in both locations."

There was a pause while they digested that.

"Does the snow in Cheshire contain exactly the same remains?" Wells asked.

"Similar," Ruth said. "I need to check the new samples coming in. We found larger samples around Clapham Junction after the explosion. We've also found that the houses in Battersea and Shakerley Manor are the centres of the earth tremors in each area."

"The sand in Cheshire could come from remaining sand deposits," Wells said. "Shakerley Mere used to be a sandpit."

"The composition of the sand is entirely different from the local sand," Derek White said.

"I don't see where any of this leads us," the naval officer said. "The possibility that the house in Battersea was built on some sort of ancient seabed with dinosaur prawns, and that the manor has something similar, but not exactly the same, is interesting but doesn't really help us. Couldn't there be an ancient seabed under Cheshire, too?"

"I don't know," Ruth said. She'd have to look into that. "But even if there was, it'd be strange that it'd somehow found its way into the snow."

A few of those in the meeting nodded at this.

"There are also reports of strange creatures in London and around the mere," she said.

"A panther's been seen in London. It seems to have been trained," Best said. "But the reports from Cheshire haven't been confirmed."

"I saw—"

Best interrupted her. "You and your boyfriend claim to have seen shadows in the middle of the night, but in daylight, nothing could be found. We've got men camped around the lake right now. If there was anything there, they would've seen it."

"The shadow smashed a hole twice the size of my head through the wooden panelling of the dining room," she said.

"Somebody broke the panelling," Best said. "But there's no indication it was a monster."

The meeting moved on, and Ruth wondered what Jack had actually seen in Battersea.

"What about the occult connection?" the home secretary asked.

Best shook his head. "We can't see any connection." He cleared his throat. "Leander Amis appears to have been rather eccentric; a trait that's been shown by members of parliament before."

Everybody in the room knew about the revelations the month before regarding the strange sex life of a well-known backbencher.

"But the report on Amis's death states he was sacrificed in a black magic ceremony," the home secretary said.

"It may be a weird cult, but I think it's much more likely that it's just a distraction. An attempt to have us looking in the wrong direction," the head of MI6 said.

"And that one of the suspects is an occultist."

"That could be another distraction. It's possible that the abduction was staged," Best said. "Of course, we've checked on local occult groups but haven't found any leads."

"Do you think it was staged?" the home secretary asked.

"One of our operatives thinks not, but the majority of the police at the scene think it likely," Best replied. "Or at least, a falling out amongst criminals."

"What about Dr Lee? Can he speak their language?" Wells asked.

"Some," Best said. "He's been attempting to decipher it by himself. His wound is superficial, and we're planning to allow him to continue with this."

The home secretary nodded. "It's a strange business. But no one has mentioned the aims of the group. What do they want?"

"They've not made any demands," Wells said. "One of the MI5 operatives has suggested that a man named Olney may be the mastermind."

"We suspect that they're not terrorists," Best said. "At least, not conventional ones. We believe they're working for a foreign government, and that they may have been chosen from a remote region of their country because using a rare dialect could help them maintain secrecy." He paused for breath and then continued. "After the explosion in

Battersea, we're concerned that a foreign power is planning to test a new type of weapon, and that the test may take place at sunrise, tomorrow morning."

"Why?" the home secretary asked.

Best shrugged. "To create chaos and destabilise our country, perhaps. At the moment, we don't know."

There was a moment's silence in the room, and then all those present began speaking at the same time.

The home secretary spoke over the noise, and gradually the room quietened. "Do you think the explosion in Battersea was a weapon test gone wrong?"

"It was too big to be a gas explosion. The fire was too fierce. We think it was some sort of weapon," Best said. "But we don't know whether the blast was intentional or not."

"And you think this might happen at Shakerley?" the home secretary asked.

"It's possible, although we're checking out locations in south London, too," Best said. "According to Dr Lee, Shakerley will be the location of the catastrophic incident."

"Do you believe Lee's story?" the home secretary asked.

"It fits with other things we've found. A diary was retrieved from the house in Battersea. The entry for this Sunday is in the foreign language, but it says Shakerley in English.

"And the frequency of earth tremors has increased there, as have new deposits of sand. It's now falling directly from the sky, whether it's snowing or not. Something is definitely happening.

"We believe the country is facing a serious threat. Whether the threat manifests itself in Cheshire or in London, we can't be sure, but we need to be prepared at both locations. I suggest that the military is sent to Shakerley,"

The home secretary nodded. "The Counter Terrorism Unit will be in charge of the operation, at least for now, but the military will be sent for support. Let me introduce Rear Admiral Benson to those who don't know him." Turning to the admiral, she continued. "How quickly can you assemble a team?"

"I have a unit of the Special Boat Service that can be there this evening."

Ruth listened, very alert. The SBS was Jack's old unit, before he joined MI5. Perhaps Jack knew the admiral.

"815 Naval Air Squadron can accompany them. We may need further land and air support."

"You can have whatever you need," the home secretary said.

"I also want a translator. Give me Dr Lee."

"He's under arrest," Wells said. "But I agree that he's probably the best choice."

"I want Ms Hardy, too," the admiral said.

"Me?" Ruth was surprised after the apparent dismissal of her ideas.

"If we're up against giant prawns, I want an expert opinion at hand."

## 19

Jack's phone rang. He didn't want to answer. He was on the street outside his London flat; it was getting dark, and he'd literally just arrived back from a series of meetings and was hoping for a shower and some rest.

"Hello, Alice," he said.

"Jack, the police have found the grey van. It was abandoned at a service station on the M1, just north of London."

"So they may be going up north?"

"Perhaps. We're putting your team there. We want you to head straight to Shakerley, just in case."

Turning round, he walked back to his car.

"Any clues?"

"Assault rifles, stolen. All with ammunition. And the body of the getaway driver. He'd been shot in the head."

"Nice. Payment for his services. What do the police have on him?"

Jack started his car.

"A history of petty theft and violence. Oh, and Steel Badge is in play." Alice hung up.

It was code—Jack could legally ignore the speed limit.

He was tired when he reached the M1, but he was used to that. At least he could drive fast, and fog and black ice had reduced the number of motorists. People had better things to do than endanger themselves driving on a freezing night. The faster he got there, the faster he could get back, if it turned out to be nothing. If he had the chance, he'd kill Angel, too. The execution of Bonnie was unbearable. As his thoughts turned to her, he found his foot pressing hard on the accelerator. He didn't care. The sooner he found the killers, the better.

Then there was Dr Lee. Jack wasn't sure what to make of the man. He'd recovered from the shot—luckily for him, it'd been no more than a bloody graze—and he'd been forthcoming with the police. He'd be sent north for his translation skills. It wasn't as if he'd escape—not with the police and military presence, but most of the information had been too woo for the police. Especially the psychic stuff. Ruth had ridiculed this part of his story, but Jack suspected there was more to life than what most people thought, and he withheld his judgement on some of what the man had said, although talk of aliens seemed to be going too far.

Lee had also mentioned two types of creatures working for the killers: hunters and warriors. Ruth had picked up on that. Was the lizard at the lake a warrior? She was already convinced there was more than one. If true, it didn't bode well for the operation. The panther was clearly a hunter. It seemed to have tracked the suspects from Clapham Junction to Battersea Park. His superiors were still in denial, but these things were real and deadly. Ruth had outlined the meeting to him. He was pleased his old unit was involved, and confident they could deal with any squad of foreign killers.

It was almost seven o'clock when he reached the section of the motorway adjoining Shakerley Manor. The motorway lights shone through the fog, allowing him to see Pete's car parked on the hard shoulder, about three hundred yards ahead. Jack knew a police firearms unit of six marksmen was already at the manor, as well as about twenty regular police officers. They were awaiting further instructions. He stopped and got out of his car, pulling up his jacket collar. This was close to where he and Ruth had escaped the lizard.

Pete leant against his car. As usual, he was surrounded by a cloud of smoke. Both boot and bonnet were wide open. Claire was at the next motorway exit in case the targets took that route. Randall waited to the south at the Middlewich turn-off. Their job was to observe and follow if the killers came north along a more conventional route instead of accessing Shakerley from the motorway. Randall had insisted the killers wouldn't stand a chance, but Jack wasn't so sure.

After twenty minutes, it started to snow again. Jack was about to get back into his car when a white van approached, and he pretended to be checking the engine. It stopped on the hard shoulder about eighty yards in front of him. Angel and the shooter from London climbed out of the van, pulling a woman behind them. It looked like Blake. She walked as if she were drugged. One of the men slapped her. This was it.

"Base," Jack said as the panther jumped out of the van. "I have contact. Angel Provost and the other shooter I saw by Rosery Gate—perhaps it's Olney. They have the hostage. The panther's here, too."

The men rushed up the embankment, pulling the woman with them. Jack could no longer see the black panther.

"I'll inform the police," Alice said. "How long will it take them to get to your side of the mere?"

"Fifteen minutes if they run."

"Hopefully they'll be in place, and the targets will be walking into a trap," Alice said. "Observe the encounter, but remain concealed."

"Roger that, Alice."

Aware that his cover might already have gone, Jack continued to look under the bonnet of the car while the men climbed over the fence at the top of the embankment. Pete appeared to be searching for something in the back of his car.

They disappeared down the slope on the other side, and Pete sprinted towards them, but Jack was closer and reached the top of the ridge first. Dropping on hands and knees, he crawled the final part of the way and looked over. Pete soon joined him. They watched the men run towards a line of trees; they were slowed by the hostage.

"If only we had guns and were allowed to use them," Pete said.

"Let the police shoot them full of bullets," Jack said. But privately, he agreed.

"Do you think they can handle it?" Pete asked.

Jack shrugged. "There're only two of them, but they're professionals. I hate to admit it, but Angel was one of the best."

"Even when he was on drugs?"

"They made him more violent."

"Was he in your squadron?"

"Yes."

Jack realised he wanted vengeance. He wanted it for Bonnie and Steve. If he'd killed Angel in the mountains, after he'd executed that family, his friends would still be alive. But there was no way he could have seen the future. If his supervisors in MI5 could look inside his head right now, they'd throw him out of the service without a second thought. But he was more worried what Ruth might think of him.

When the men had almost reached the wooded area, Jack and Pete climbed over the fence and quickly crawled down the slope to a depression in the ground. They waited while the police trap was sprung.

A police officer moved in the wood. He spoke through a megaphone.

"You're surrounded! Drop your weapons!"

Jack and Pete edged closer. The darkness and the fog gave cover. Jack could just see Angel through the trees. He'd put his pistol to Blake's head.

"If you shoot, she's dead," Olney said.

Jack was sure it was him. His accent was strong.

"You can't get away. Let her go, and then put your weapons on the ground," the police officer said.

Jack counted four police marksmen in the trees; he couldn't see the other two. Perhaps they were hidden deeper in the woods. There were regular police, too, further back. He continued to edge forwards through the long grass.

Olney whistled, and one of the police marksmen cried out and dropped to the ground, a dark shape covering him. Jack quietly cursed, he'd almost forgotten the panther. About ten seconds later another man screamed. It was moving fast under the cover of darkness.

More shots came from the woods, and from the way the killers dragged Blake to the mere, Jack no longer had any doubts that she was really their prisoner; whether they'd once been colleagues and the relationship had soured, he couldn't be sure. Jack and Pete followed them into the wooded area, carefully keeping their distance. For a second time, it wasn't going well for the police. They'd underestimated the killers again. But his orders were to observe. Nothing more. More shots were exchanged, and Olney shot another armed officer dead. Angel fired at the fourth, forcing him to take cover behind a tree.

Pete spoke to Thames House, then hung up. "The word's still to observe. Two more police shooters are coming from the manor."

Jack frowned. He had no idea why they were there and not here. There were more shots and shouts. Then silence came to the woods again, apart from the odd shouted instruction from the police.

"What's happening?" Pete asked.

"The panther's got the last shooter," Jack said.

"You can't be sure," Pete whispered. "We can't see a thing."

"I'm sure."

Despite the darkness within the woods, light from the full moon shone through in some places. Jack saw movement ahead of them. The killers moved fast towards the lake, not having to worry about being shot by the regular police. As they walked past an injured officer, Olney shot him to make sure he was dead.

Pete quietly cursed.

Jack nodded. They were dealing with scum. A police van raced around the lake, but the sight of it gave him no confidence. It would be there in less than half a minute, but neither of the killers appeared to care. They stood by the lake. Angel checked his pistol; Olney spoke on the phone.

What would his call bring? Jack prayed it wasn't the thing that had attacked him in the manor. That would make the panther look like a pet cat.

Olney whistled.

they'd throw him out of the service without a second thought. But he was more worried what Ruth might think of him.

When the men had almost reached the wooded area, Jack and Pete climbed over the fence and quickly crawled down the slope to a depression in the ground. They waited while the police trap was sprung.

A police officer moved in the wood. He spoke through a megaphone.

"You're surrounded! Drop your weapons!"

Jack and Pete edged closer. The darkness and the fog gave cover. Jack could just see Angel through the trees. He'd put his pistol to Blake's head.

"If you shoot, she's dead," Olney said.

Jack was sure it was him. His accent was strong.

"You can't get away. Let her go, and then put your weapons on the ground," the police officer said.

Jack counted four police marksmen in the trees; he couldn't see the other two. Perhaps they were hidden deeper in the woods. There were regular police, too, further back. He continued to edge forwards through the long grass.

Olney whistled, and one of the police marksmen cried out and dropped to the ground, a dark shape covering him. Jack quietly cursed, he'd almost forgotten the panther. About ten seconds later another man screamed. It was moving fast under the cover of darkness.

More shots came from the woods, and from the way the killers dragged Blake to the mere, Jack no longer had any doubts that she was really their prisoner; whether they'd once been colleagues and the relationship had soured, he couldn't be sure. Jack and Pete followed them into the wooded area, carefully keeping their distance. For a second time, it wasn't going well for the police. They'd underestimated the killers again. But his orders were to observe. Nothing more. More shots were exchanged, and Olney shot another armed officer dead. Angel fired at the fourth, forcing him to take cover behind a tree.

Pete spoke to Thames House, then hung up. "The word's still to observe. Two more police shooters are coming from the manor."

Jack frowned. He had no idea why they were there and not here. There were more shots and shouts. Then silence came to the woods again, apart from the odd shouted instruction from the police.

"What's happening?" Pete asked.

"The panther's got the last shooter," Jack said.

"You can't be sure," Pete whispered. "We can't see a thing."

"I'm sure."

Despite the darkness within the woods, light from the full moon shone through in some places. Jack saw movement ahead of them. The killers moved fast towards the lake, not having to worry about being shot by the regular police. As they walked past an injured officer, Olney shot him to make sure he was dead.

Pete quietly cursed.

Jack nodded. They were dealing with scum. A police van raced around the lake, but the sight of it gave him no confidence. It would be there in less than half a minute, but neither of the killers appeared to care. They stood by the lake. Angel checked his pistol; Olney spoke on the phone.

What would his call bring? Jack prayed it wasn't the thing that had attacked him in the manor. That would make the panther look like a pet cat.

Olney whistled.

"Where is it?" Pete whispered, looking around frantically.

"Good question." It was the perfect environment for a panther to hunt. Jack stared towards the lake, wondering what the killers were doing there. He couldn't see anything with the fog over the lake.

"Are we just going to stay here and watch them kill the police?" Pete asked.

"Those are our orders." *Or near enough,* Jack thought.

Olney aimed his pistol towards the approaching van. It clicked, and he tossed it away.

"Out of ammo," Jack whispered. "But I don't like that he's so casual about throwing away a weapon like that."

"Better for us."

"Yes, but it's as if he's got bigger things to think about."

"A bomb?" Pete asked.

"I don't know," Jack said. Some sort of terrorist demands, along with the threat of a bombing, was a possibility. But what they could blow up in the middle of the countryside, he had no idea. He watched Olney carefully; he appeared professional, but wasting weapons wasn't something a professional would do unless he had good reason. "When the other's empty, we can move in."

Pete grinned. "Aren't we observing?"

Jack shrugged.

"There's still the panther," Pete said.

"True."

The police van stopped, and officers rushed out of the back. Seconds later, there was another scream.

"What is that thing? Pete said. "It's taking out half the police force."

"A hunter," Jack replied. "A good one. I think it was waiting in a tree."

So much for the killers stepping into a police trap.

"Jack, what's happening?" It was Alice.

"Four or five marksmen are dead. And some of the regulars. The panther's hunting in the woods. The police trap has fallen apart, and we're in danger, too. I request permission for us to arm ourselves."

"Are there any police marksmen left?"

"One or two, but I don't rate their chances. The killers are some of the best I've seen." A shot rang out, and one of the men went down. Angel lowered his pistol.

"What was that?" Alice asked.

"Angel killed another," Jack said. He paused to watch the killers. "They're doing something on the shore of the lake."

"What?"

"We're too far back to see clearly. Without a weapon, I can't attempt to get closer."

"Jack, you're both authorised to do whatever you have to to stop them. We won't hold you accountable for their deaths. But one thing, Jack—I don't want you or Pete to risk your lives."

"That's part of the job, Alice. And they're being pretty free with the killing. How long till the boat squadron arrives?"

"Two hours."

He cursed. He wanted them right now; this meant they'd arrive at ten o'clock.

"Jack, do what you can, but stay safe." Alice hung up.

"We've been authorised to use weapons," Jack said. "If we can get any."

They moved through the trees, getting closer to one of the assault rifles. The woman saw them, and she reached for Angel's gun. The gun fired into the ground.

"What's she doing?" Pete said.

"I think she's trying to help us," Jack said. "She's spending his ammo."

The gun clicked.

"It's empty," Jack said.

He cringed when Angel punched the woman in the head, and she went straight down.

"Look!" Pete said.

Jack had already seen the boat moving through the fog towards the shore.

"They're on the island," Pete said. "In the ruined tower. No wonder nobody found any sign of them."

Jack agreed. There was nowhere to hide on the other island. All it had was grass and a few trees. The boat reached the shore, and Angel lifted the apparently unconscious woman on board, climbing in after her. Jack could reach them in seven or eight seconds if he sprinted, but the assault rifle was too far in the wrong direction. If he was going to do anything, he'd have to take the risk they didn't have a weapon in the boat.

"Let's take them, Jack," Pete said. "I know you were special forces, and I was just a squaddy, but I can handle myself."

Jack shook his head, regretting his earlier comment about moving in. Pete was a good guy, and he was handy in a fight, but these men were professional killers. "It's too risky. The panther's practically invisible."

"I saw a shadow moving near the police. I think we can make it."

Olney started to climb inside.

"Let them go," Jack said. "We'll get them later." He was confident in his skills, and he believed he could take on either of these men, but not both. And as much as he liked Pete, his fighting skills were not up to this.

"You're not my commanding officer, Jack. And why should your old unit get all the glory?"

Pete sprinted towards the boat, and Jack cursed. He had no choice but to follow, but he was several yards behind. He tried to convince his friend again, but Pete wasn't listening. Jack drew his knife. He always carried it—it was something that either no one in MI5 had ever noticed, or something that had been purposely overlooked by his superiors.

Olney had stepped away from the boat and was watching them approach. Pete tried to tackle the man around the neck, but the killer slipped out, elbowing him and gaining space. Angel jumped out of the boat.

"Go! I can deal with these nuisances."

Angel reluctantly got back in the boat, and the boatman took the boat out into the lake.

Jack had almost reached Pete, who was trying to take the man down, but he wasn't as practised as Jack was at this kind of thing. Before Jack could reach them, Olney twisted free and put Pete in a headlock. Jack knew the move. He'd killed men in action using it.

"Let him go, Olney," Jack said.

The man looked up. "So? You know my name."

Olney broke his neck and pushed him away. Pete lay dead on the frozen ground. The man glanced at the boat, but it was now disappearing into the fog.

"You're dead!" Jack said. He approached Olney with his knife in hand.

The man said something in a foreign language, and then he attacked. He knocked Jack's knife away with a move that took him by surprise. He was too fast. Within seconds, Jack realised he'd made a mistake. For the first time in a long time, he was fighting someone better than him. And stronger. Jack was an expert grappler, but this man was choking him, and he was losing consciousness.

A shot came from the trees. Olney seemed to curse in his language. He pushed him away. Jack lay in the shallow water seeing stars and gasping for breath. He heard movement near him, and through pure effort of will, he forced himself to sit up.

He watched the killer wade into the frigid water and swim into the darkness.

Then Jack passed out.

## 20

Amelia woke up cold and damp, her bruised lips still tasting of the anaesthetic from the sodden rag that the man called Angel had pushed in her mouth. It'd been slowly wearing off since they'd slapped her awake and dragged her from the van, but she still felt nauseous. She remembered the punch—the side of her face was still sore.

Shivering, she slowly sat up on an old bed. The springs beneath her squeaked as she moved. She'd not been there long. Her hands were bound in front of her, but her feet were free. She stood. The only light came from a candle burning on a saucer on the floor; it flickered as a cold breeze blew through an open window high on the wall. There was no furniture apart from the bed.

She walked unsteadily across the room and turned the door handle. It was locked. She then looked at the old wooden door and the arched doorway, touching the damp stone wall that curved inwards around her. It seemed like she was in the turret of an old castle.

Deciding to try to reach the small window, she pulled the bed underneath it and stood on it. It was still too high.

Seeing a large, rusty nail beneath the window, she hooked the rope between her wrists over it and pulled, pleased she regularly worked out. Slowly, she edged up to the window. There was a full moon, but it was hard to see because of the fog. However, she saw water around her. She seemed to be on an island in a lake. Looking up, she saw that she was near the top of a tower. Lowering herself slightly, she began to rub the rope over the long nail. It would take time to cut through the rope, but she had nothing else to do. Eventually, with the combination of her rubbing the rope against the nail and her body weight, she began to cut through the material.

About twenty minutes later, she dropped back onto the bed below, her hands free. She pushed the bed back and sat down to consider what she could do. Escaping through the window was dangerous, and she'd rather not try. The outer wall had places to grip, but it was damp, and a fall from this height could easily mean a broken leg or worse. For several minutes Amelia sat on the bed feeling sorry for herself. But however justified her feelings were, they wouldn't help. She was used to brainstorming problems, and she began by mentally listing her strengths. Although they'd stolen her phone, she had other ways of communicating.

She could ask her guides, but all they could do was give advice; they couldn't offer practical help, apart from alerting her to things in her environment. She could contact the witch again, but the thought of it scared her, and she doubted she'd be able to offer any practical help either. She could attempt to contact Luke. In the past, she'd reached out telepathically to other people, but Luke was so intellectual, and dense energetically, that she was worried he'd either unconsciously reject any attempt she made, or not notice at all. But it was worth a try.

She sat on the bed and closed her eyes, thinking about Luke Lee, a man she'd known for a day but felt like she'd known for years. She wanted to tell him where she was. As she lay on the bed, she thought about him, and at the same time formed an image of the tower in her mind.

*"Luke, I'm here."*

Several seconds later, she became aware of his presence. He was stressed and somewhere with bright lights. He'd either be in a hospital or a police station. Feeling her concentration drift, she again focussed on the feeling of danger as she visualised the old tower. But he cut contact—probably unconsciously. To receive messages in this way was threatening for most people. She was unsure if anything had reached his conscious mind.

Shivering as a cold blast of wind blew through the window, she opened her eyes and thought about all of the people she'd met in connection with the strange events. The man Angel had called Sergeant Ross came to mind. There was an emotional intensity in him. Without any inner debate, she focussed on the unknown man and their few seconds of contact. Angel had said that he worked for the Security Service; he'd certainly been intent on protecting the woman called Bonnie, and the thought of the woman's death gave her a burst of emotion. Amelia breathed deeply. She felt his presence. He was in some dark, damp place like her. Breathing deeply, and feeling energy flowing through her body, she spoke the inner language. More than a thought, she projected her inner speech towards him.

*"Help me!"*

He was aware of her.

She showed him the tower and her captivity, and she sensed recognition. He was somewhere close. Feeling her excitement building, she slowed her breathing. She repeated her message, but this time she expressed not personal danger but danger to the country. She shared the vision that had been repeating itself in her dreams, and even in some waking moments over the past few days—a vision of a burning Earth. This time, she felt a stronger response. Unsure what to do next, she visualised the upper floor where she was being held. She felt his surprise, and then he was gone. For a few minutes she relaxed; she'd done what she could.

Turning her attention to the tower itself, she opened her inner senses and listened. There was something she didn't like, perhaps a person. The feeling came from somewhere deeper in the tower. Noises outside distracted her, and she opened her eyes. She held her hands together, hoping that in the low light, her captor wouldn't notice the cut rope.

The door swung open. "You," she said. It was Angel. This time without the creature. She still felt the bruises he'd given her. He'd been on drugs when he'd kidnapped her. Now he was sweating despite the cold. She'd dealt with drug addicts at work—he looked like he was suffering from withdrawal. He stared at her from the doorway, making her feel uneasy. "Where am I?" she asked.

"It doesn't matter." His voice was flat. "You're staying here now."

She shivered at his coldness and the implied permanence of her location.

He spoke on his phone. "She's awake." She strained to hear the reply but couldn't.

"Why did you take me, Angel?"

His eyes widened slightly when she said his name, but he didn't answer. She needed to know more, and as he began to leave the room she thought desperately of a way to engage him in conversation. She noticed a cross around his neck and an angel tattooed on his throat. As he was closing the door, she spoke.

"Why an angel?" She couldn't think of anything else to say.

He stared at her and reflexively touched his neck. She tried to keep calm under his gaze, and she hoped that she hadn't touched some unseen nerve or childhood trauma. But she knew she needed to touch something inside him, just hopefully without triggering a violent reaction.

"You know nothing about me."

"That's almost true."

He paused.

"You serve people who seek to undermine the security of this country."

"I serve no one."

"You do what you're told." He seemed to be blanking her out again. "You kill for money."

"So?" he said. He stared at her without speaking.

She felt empathically for his emotions; they were dulled. "Why me?"

He didn't answer.

"Do you know your boss uses black magic?"

"It's not real."

She shook her head. "It's real."

His eyes narrowed. "What would you know about it?"

"I've studied the subject."

She spoke with conviction, and she saw she'd made some impression. Perhaps he already knew that all was not right with his employers, but his temper was rising, and she had no doubt this man was very dangerous. Seeking to stem his anger, she spoke again.

"Tell me about the panther." She prayed that it wouldn't walk through the door when he opened it.

He tensed.

"She loves you," Amelia said.

She'd seen them together, and she knew something of animals. For the first time, the killer softened, and she breathed out in relief. She'd guessed right about their bond.

"She's a huntress," she said. This was something she'd learnt from the witch.

His mouth opened, and then he nodded. "She is." He studied her for several seconds. "You're different from the others." Then he left the room.

Now Amelia had new questions. Who were the others? And where were they? She prayed that the answer was not at the bottom of the lake.

As soon as he'd gone, she again attempted to contact Sergeant Ross. She sensed he was close, and this time she imagined the killer who had just left the room. For a moment she felt a flicker of emotion, and then it was gone. But she knew that for a brief moment she'd connected, and that the image of the killer stirred some emotion within him.

A shout from outside disturbed her thoughts. Quickly pulling the bed back to the window, Amelia pulled herself up using the old nail. Then, finding a small toehold, she pushed further up, taking care not to skewer herself on the rusty nail, until she could lean into the window space in the thick wall. She saw figures moving in the fog. Someone was splashing in the lake. It looked like a woman. A man rushed into the shallow water and grabbed hold of her. A baby cried. Amelia had no idea why they would be swimming in a freezing lake. She lowered herself and sat on the bed, puzzled by the woman's appearance.

About fifteen minutes later, she started when the door flew open and slammed against the stone wall. Angel pulled the woman and child into the room. Then, without a word, he left. The woman was soaked and shivering. She staggered across the room, and Amelia caught her, stopping her from falling. The baby was strapped to the woman's back. Water dripped onto the stone floor, forming pools around the woman's feet.

"Who are you?" Amelia asked.

"Molly Lee. This is my son."

## 21

Jack lay on the shore of the lake. It was dark, and for several seconds he was unsure where he was. He was wet, and he was aware of water lapping around him. Something wasn't right, but he couldn't place it. He listened. Then he felt it again. A vibration disturbed the lake.

"You alright, mate?" A police constable stood over him.

Jack sat up slowly and rubbed his neck. He was sore and still felt disoriented, but his memories of the incident returned. Pete's body lay nearby.

"Inspector Gully wants to speak to you. He's in the manor. Do you need help walking?"

The thought of Gully, warm inside the manor while his men were dying outside on the frozen ground, snapped him back to reality.

"I'm okay."

He stood, still feeling light-headed, and walked over to where Pete lay. He paused for several seconds, thinking of his lost comrades: Bonnie, Steve, and now Pete. As with the rest of the team, he knew almost nothing about Pete's personal life. Yet after Ruth, these were the people he cared most about in the world. And now they were being killed by a team of assassins.

Jack walked past the police officers who were going through the scene of carnage and picked up a submachine gun piled up with other weapons by the van.

"Inspector Gully gave orders that no one touch the guns," a constable said.

"I'll give it to him myself."

The constable seemed unsure what to do, and Jack walked back along the path. It was dark; he wasn't walking through the woods unarmed, not with the panther free. And perhaps other things, too. As he walked, he thought about what was happening. The killers were gathering here. There must be a reason. What could they do from a ruined tower on an island in the middle of a lake?

And what had caused the vibration?

He decided that there must be something in the lake. When the Naval Air Squadron arrived, they needed to search the lake bed. The lizard had come from and gone back to the mere. This was the weirdest operation he'd taken part in. He shivered and walked faster, glancing up at the trees as he moved through them.

Police milled around the manor, and they stared at him as he walked in, but no one challenged him. He found Inspector Gully in the library.

"What's that?" Gully asked.

"A Heckler and Koch MP5," Jack said, instantly disliking the man.

"That's not what I meant. I left instructions that nobody pick those up. You're interfering with my investigation."

"Investigation? We're under attack." Jack handed the weapon to a constable wearing gloves. "There's also a panther that's hunting and killing your men."

"I know what's happening. I've been fully briefed. And I don't appreciate your interference."

"We were trying to stop the killers escape," Jack said.

"And look what happened. Ten of my men are dead, eleven including your colleague. Understand this: I'm in charge of this operation, and I'm asking you not to get involved. The Security Service is here to observe, not participate. You're to report to your commanding officer on the outer perimeter."

"Outer perimeter?"

"Your colleagues in MI5 are observing from the outer perimeter I set up half a kilometre away with groups of local police. I want you to join them."

Jack raised his eyebrows. The man didn't seem to understand what he was facing.

"I'm going to clean up and rest." Jack felt better than he looked, but he'd use any excuse to stay. He was going to get these killers.

The inspector looked at the blood and dirt on his clothes and nodded. "You can rest upstairs. I'll send a medic up, but I request that you remain inside the manor."

"There's another predator hunting in the woods," Jack said.

"I've heard your theories on monsters from the merc. What exactly happened?"

Jack described what he'd heard and seen, but the man hardly listened.

"Fine. Clean up and make yourself a coffee, but don't interfere with my operation."

"One more thing," Jack said. "There's something under the lake. I felt the vibrations. Possibly a machine."

"A machine under the lake?" Gully looked incredulous.

The inspector shook his head and returned to his work without another word.

Jack resisted telling him that it wouldn't be his operation for much longer. Soon, he hoped, and then someone of competence could take over. He left the room and climbed the stairs. By the time he reached the landing, he was already explaining the situation to Alice at Thames House.

"Jack, we want you to remain at the scene until the military arrive. Observe everything. I'll organise it so Inspector Gully receives instructions that you are to remain and observe unhindered."

"Thanks, Alice. How long before the military arrives?"

"One hour thirty minutes. Get some sleep first."

He needed a rest and doubted whether much would happen by then. A medic checked him over in the main bedroom but found nothing more than cuts and bruises. Once he'd gone, Jack lay on the bed, setting his alarm for thirty minutes. He fell straight into a deep sleep.

Waking up half an hour later, he decided to explore the secret passages. He knew they went upstairs because he'd seen the narrow set of stairs, but the last time he'd been escaping from a giant lizard. For the next few minutes, Jack felt and pushed the wooden panelling on the walls. Noticing that the inner wall on the side of the door was particularly thick, he searched it more carefully. A few more minutes passed before he found a panel that slid back. Reaching inside, he found a lever and pushed. The door slid open, and he stepped inside, using his phone light to help navigate along the passage. It was a straight line leading to the set of steep steps. He half expected to find peepholes, but there was nothing.

At the top of the steps was a small space with brick benches. It looked like it'd been designed to accommodate three of four people. He spent some time searching for any more hidden levers or holes but found nothing. The hiding space seemed to have been unused for a long time. Next he made his way downstairs. The steps were tight, and he smelt dust he'd dislodged. At the bottom of the steps, he recognised the part of the passage where he'd escaped the monster. To his left was the passage to the coal bunker, which he quickly explored. It was short and ended in a small room. He had to crouch as he entered it. In the centre of the wall was a large lever; above it was a peephole. On opening it, he smelt the coal clearly, but it was stacked against the door, making it unusable.

A little disappointed that he'd found nothing but constricted passages, he made his way past the dining room, stopping at the broken door that opened onto the hall. A policewoman cried out as he half fell through the hole into the dimly lit hallway.

"I'm sorry," Jack said, unable to resist a grin. "Have you seen the inspector?"

"He's still in the library," she said. "And not happy."

"Who is?"

Brushing what dirt he could from his clothes, as he walked to the library, he noticed that police reinforcements had arrived. On entering the library, he saw Gully speaking on the phone. The police officer had been right; he wasn't happy. He hung up and turned to Jack.

"You have permission to observe," Gully said.

Jack didn't bother commenting on that. The military would be here in less than an hour.

"How many men do you have?" Jack asked.

"Eight marksmen and thirty regulars, but some of those regulars have firearms training; they'll be given the six assault rifles from the dead men."

"Where are they?"

"I'm positioning them at strategic points around the lake," Inspector Gully said.

Jack tried to imagine what Gully thought were strategic points.

"I think fourteen firearms officers and twenty-four regular officers can handle two gunmen."

"It isn't always numbers that wins the day," Jack said. "I'm sure your officers are well-trained, but the people they're up against are not regular gunmen. One was special forces, and the other may be foreign special forces." In fact, Jack was sure of it. "Have you shot the panther yet?"

"Not yet. Now, if you'll excuse me, I'm busy."

Jack went to one of the large windows and looked out to the lake while Gully gave orders. For several seconds, he had the strange feeling that Amelia Blake was trying to speak to him—that she was in trouble. And then the feeling was gone. He rubbed his head, wondering whether he'd hit it harder than he thought.

Pushing the thought aside, he focussed again on the police operation. Twenty-eight officers, including all those with guns, moved into positions around the lake, leaving ten unarmed police officers inside the manor, most of whom were involved in coordinating the men. It seemed that the inspector believed that Olney had most likely drowned, and that they were dealing with at most two men holed up in the tower, as well as the hostage. He doubted that the killer had drowned—he was too tough. But the man might be weakened after swimming over a hundred yards in frigid water.

A shot came from the lake.

Jack sighed. He knew combat was never convenient, but he'd really hoped they'd wait until the military had arrived. It was starting again, and the police were not prepared.

## 22

The attack started.

Jack stood in the library, unable to do more than observe the incompetence.

Shots came from several locations around the lake, too many for this to be the work of two or three men. A police officer answered a call over the radio.

"Two men are dead, sir," he reported.

"How?" the Inspector Gully asked.

"Something cut them up bad. There's pieces of them all along the shore." The man's voice was shaky as he spoke. "There's something in the water..."

More losses were reported, and some of the units didn't respond. Jack had a bad feeling about this. "Get them out of there," he said.

"You're observing," Gully said.

Jack wished he'd kept the assault rifle. Looking around the room, he saw no spare weapons. The only option seemed to be the shotguns in the cupboard. He wasn't sure the inspector knew about them, and if not, he didn't want to alert him to them too soon. They might be a last hope.

There was still half an hour until the military arrived, and twelve officers had already died that evening. And those were only the ones they knew about. The inspector tried calling for police backup, but there was nothing available. Jack wasn't surprised. It was late Saturday evening, and this place was in the middle of nowhere. A screech came from the lake, followed by a second and third. Gully stared towards the lake transfixed for several seconds, then, seeming to come awake, he started yelling orders. Jack cringed. Gully was sending men to their deaths. Small groups of men were rushing around the lake towards the sounds. Several minutes later, shouts came from all along the shores of the lake. Two more were reported dead, taking the total of known deaths to fourteen.

The police officers in the room looked distraught.

"Are there any spare weapons?" Jack asked. "Every officer needs to be armed."

The sergeant shook his head. "They're all out there." He glanced through the open french windows.

Jack went to the cupboard in the corner of the library; he couldn't wait any longer. Shotguns weren't much use against these creatures, but they were better than nothing. He opened it, relieved to find two shotguns were still there. The police had only taken away the ones they'd used against the lizard. Jack stuffed his pockets full of cartridges and took both guns, passing one to the sergeant, who quickly loaded it.

"It's not much, but it can slow them. Aim for the eyes," Jack said. The sergeant seemed grateful.

Inspector Gully looked at him but didn't speak. He seemed close to panic. Shots came from the north side of the lake, closer to the manor.

"Order all units back to the manor house," Jack said.

Gully wandered into the garden mumbling something unintelligible. This wasn't the time for a nervous breakdown.

Jack turned to a sergeant. "There's something wrong with your inspector. Recall all units. We're under attack from an armed group—not just two or three men."

The sergeant nodded. Soon the officers on the radio had sent out the order to recall all units, but only a few responded. He glanced at his watch and quietly cursed. They still had twenty-two minutes until the military arrived. Several minutes later, five police officers ran into the garden. They'd lost twenty-three officers. Fifteen police officers remained—two were armed with assault rifles.

The woman police officer stifled a cry and pointed to the lake.

About fifteen yards in front of them, two dark silhouettes emerged from the lake. The lizards walked towards them.

One of the young constables approached Jack and offered his assault rifle. "I picked this up, but I've never fired one."

Jack nodded. He offered his shotgun in exchange. "Have you ever fired one of these?"

"I'll learn."

An eight-foot lizard with tattooed skin stared at them from the bottom of the garden. Its neck frills expanded, and it screeched. Inspector Gully stood in front of it with his hands over his face. He was moaning. Three more of the monsters emerged from the mere. All of them were over seven feet tall.

"Shoot!" Jack shouted.

The marksman fired, and Jack joined him. The bullets hurt them but didn't kill. One of the things shrieked and ran straight at Inspector Gully, but Jack couldn't shoot it without hitting the inspector. It threw Gully over its back. Jack hit its lower back, but it didn't seem to notice. It dived into the mere, taking Gully with it.

Four lizards attacked the manor. One ran at the police shooter and spat. The man screamed, dropping his gun and clutching his eyes. Jack could smell the acid from where he stood. Another police officer took the assault rifle, but the thing span round and cut him in two with its tail and then leapt through one of the large windows, sending shards of glass around the room.

"Back to the hallway!" Jack shouted.

The scene was chaotic. Three black-and-green lizards were already inside the library, and the acrid smell was intense. It was the first time he'd seen them clearly. One of them pounced on the young officer who'd given Jack his rifle, slicing his leg off with its razor claws. Jack shot repeatedly at its neck, and it backed off, clutching its throat. Another officer slipped on the debris-strewn floor, and a lizard bit a chunk out of his stomach. Jack cringed and shot it repeatedly, making it step back several paces. But he could do no more to help the man.

"To the stairs!" Jack yelled.

Some of the officers heard him, and they backed into the darkened hall, towards the staircase. There were six of them: the woman police officer he'd shocked when he'd emerged from the passage; the sergeant, who was still armed with the shotgun; one of the radio operators; two other officers; and Jack. Screams came from the library as the lizards killed the men trapped inside.

"We'll hold them off from the bend near the top of the stairs," Jack said.

They ran up the stairs. Something smashed through the

front door, sending the heavy wooden door flying down the hall. Three lizards watched them from the bottom of the hallway as they stopped at the top of the stairs. Then one of them turned and reached for something on the wall in the hallway.

"It's opening the fuse box," one of the officers said.

The lights went out.

"How does an animal know how to turn off the mains?" the sergeant asked.

No one answered. The lizards gathered at the bottom of the stairs, and Jack knew what was going to happen next.

"They're going to charge," he said.

"We can't hold them off," the sergeant said.

Jack glanced at his watch. Twelve minutes until the military arrived. It was still too long.

"The first bedroom has a secret passage," he said. "The door's open. There's a hiding space at the end of the passage."

At that moment, the monsters rushed them. One of the officers lost his arm before being tossed screaming over the thing's head where he was finished off by another lizard. The second officer was just shredded.

"Up two steps!" Jack ordered. Slowly they were forced back onto the landing. He still fired at the hissing lizards, but they kept coming.

"Into the passage!" Jack shouted.

They ran into the bedroom, while he and the sergeant backed up along the landing, still shooting. Jack was impressed by the sergeant's calmness. He ignored the acid burning through his clothes and fired directly into the lizards' eyes.

Then he started to reload.

"Forget it!" Jack said.

The man threw the shotgun at an advancing lizard and ran. The creatures rushed them. One of them grabbed the barrel of Jack's rifle, seeming to grin as it took it. He followed the sergeant, slamming the bedroom door shut and shooting the bolt in place. It might give them an extra second. He felt burning on his back, and he ripped his jacket off, throwing it to the floor. It had a hole in it. He was still burning as he squeezed inside the passage.

He heard the monsters move onto the landing. They smashed through the bedroom door as if it hadn't been there. Jack closed the door to the passage behind him, praying the things would think they'd jumped from the open window. He shuffled slowly along the passage, taking off his shirt as he moved. He felt instant relief when it fell away.

The sergeant, the woman officer, and a radio operator had squeezed into the tiny stone space just above the stairs at the end of the passage. No one spoke as he joined them. Jack took out his phone. Eight minutes until the military arrived. For the first time, he dared hope that they might survive the attack. After the initial noise, there was silence in the bedroom, but Jack knew they were there. Waiting. Something was strange about these creatures. They acted as if they were intelligent—they'd turned off the power. They reminded him of commandos on an operation. The killing was too systematic.

He jumped when a piece of panelling was ripped from the wall. A long reptilian snout pushed itself inside, and it turned to look at them.

"It's grinning," the woman said.

She was right, and he shivered at the implications. He glanced again at the phone—six minutes. The head vanished, but seconds later, the monster started to rip away the wooden panelling, piece by piece.

The other monsters soon joined it. The panelling was being ripped away at an alarming speed.

"Downstairs," the sergeant said.

"No," Jack said. "We're safer here."

He pointed to where the wooden panelling ended and was replaced by stone walls. The hidden room they were in was about four yards from the end of the panelling. The monsters couldn't squeeze along the final part of the narrow stone passage, but they could spit. More sounds came from the passage below.

"They're trying to reach the stairs from the dining room," the radio operator said.

"They'll have the same problem," Jack said. "Look." He tapped the tightly winding stone stairs. "They're too big to climb the stairs. Not without dismantling the stonework. This is the safest place. Unfortunately there's no door. We need something to stop the spit."

The nearest piece of wooden panelling was pulled away, and the lizard tried to stick its large head inside the gap. The sergeant had already taken his jacket off and was holding it up; the others did the same. Shrieking and spitting, the thing tried to reach them, but it was just too big and too far away. Jack felt his fingers burn as acid touched them, but he kept hold of one side of the sergeant's jacket, and together they maintained the curtain protecting them from the spittle, which burnt holes through the jacket, and as the holes became larger, it burnt them, too.

The lizards stopped, seeming to consult. There was silence for a few minutes. Then automatic rifle fire came from outside.

"At last!" Jack said.

The thing persisted for several more seconds, and then, as if in answer to a series of shrieks and whistles, it rushed from the room. Jack edged back along the passage, scraping the spittle from his neck and arms. He froze when more glass shattered in the bedroom. Slowly breathing out, he continued to where the panelling had been ripped away. He looked around the dimly lit room. The only light came from the full moon, but it was enough to see that the room was empty.

He went to the window. The last lizard ran straight down the wall. When it neared the bottom, it leapt through the air, landing yards from the edge of the mere. Jack held the windowsill as the house shuddered and moaned to another tremor.

The lizard ran straight into the mere.

## 23

The Merlin landed and the commandos rushed into the fog, attacking an enemy Luke couldn't see. He was the last to leave the helicopter; the rotor blades had almost stopped turning when he walked towards the lake. The members of the Special Boat Service seemed to accept the carnage as something natural, but he stared in shock at the dismembered bodies lying on the ground. There was heavy gunfire by the manor. And then there was silence. Someone told him it was over.

He'd heard bits and pieces about what had happened—after being hunted through London by the panther, anything seemed possible. Not feeling like going inside yet, but unsure where to go, Luke walked along the shore. A half-submerged body of a man stuck out from the water. He changed direction and walked towards the trees. The thirty-two members of the Special Boat Service moving silently around the grounds gave him confidence. The two smaller Wildcat helicopters had taken to the air again and were circling the lake. Behind him, the pair of Merlin helicopters now sat still and were being attended to by members of the 815 Naval Air Squadron.

Then, something moved on the ground in front of him, and he froze. In the darkness, he could only see it moving closer; he couldn't make out what it was. He imagined a detached limb crawling towards him, and looking around, he realised he'd wandered away from the others. He was tempted to walk quickly to the manor, but instead, he forced himself to shine his phone torch on the ground.

A silver-and-blue lobster crawled towards him.

Perhaps someone was breeding them locally. He knew that Ruth Hardy, the woman he'd spoken to in the Merlin, was a zoologist. And although she wouldn't confirm it, he suspected she worked for the Security Service, too. He picked it up, carefully avoiding the claws.

"You're wanted in the manor," a man said.

He'd not heard the marine corporal approach. The man looked at the lobster and then left. Luke walked back towards the manor. The light of the full moon diffused through the fog, and he could see enough to avoid standing on any of the bodies. As he got closer to the manor, his thoughts returned to his work. Since his arrest, he'd continued to decipher the language. With the help of the notebook from the house in Battersea, and from Amelia's partial translation, it was beginning to come together. He could now form basic sentences.

He looked up when a tough-looking man wearing blood-stained clothes almost bumped into him as he walked through the front door.

"Dr Lee?"

Luke nodded. There was something familiar about him.

The man looked at the struggling lobster. "We're having

a meeting to discuss what we know about the terrorists. We'd like to have your thoughts."

Luke followed the man into the library, which was clearly the command centre, too.

Ruth Hardy's eyes opened wide when she saw the lobster. "Where did you find that?"

"By the woods. I don't know how it got there. It's a long way from the sea."

He walked over the fragments of glass and pieces of broken furniture covering the library floor to a scratched wooden table which several people sat around. He put it on the table, and Ruth examined it.

A man in a police uniform sat at the head of the table. Luke had seen him inside the helicopter, but they hadn't spoken.

"Dr Lee," the man said. "I'm Superintendent Dale of the Counter Terrorism Unit, and I'm in charge of negotiations." He gestured to a marine officer. "Captain Willis of the Special Boat Service is in charge of the military side of the operation." The man in blood-splattered clothes was also at the table. Luke suddenly recognised him. It was the man he'd spoken to in Battersea Park—after he'd been shot. Perhaps he was from the Security Service, too. The feeling he gave off was martial, but he wore civilian clothes. "You know Ruth Hardy."

She was examining the lobster. "The antennae are wrong. Too short. And the eyes are not right."

"What does this mean?" Captain Willis asked.

"I don't know," she said, shaking her head. "But it shouldn't be here." She picked it up. "Look at those." She pointed at darker markings on its shell. "Burns. And the shell's cracked here. It's had a rough time."

"So have we," the bloodstained man said.

She glanced at him with a look of concern. "I know." She put the lobster in a box on the floor and sat down.

"Jack, what the hell happened?" Captain Willis asked the bloody man.

Jack told the story of the attack, and Luke listened carefully. If it hadn't been for the scene of destruction, he might not have believed what he heard.

"Do you have anything to add, Dr Lee?" Superintendent Dale asked.

Luke had been preparing to speak. "I've made progress deciphering their language. I still can't identify any similar language, but with help from Amelia Blake, and the aid of the notebooks I found in Battersea, I'm now able to understand simple sentences at least."

"That could be helpful," Superintendent Dale said. "Anything else?"

Luke remembered the weird summoning Amelia had held. He described it, realising how odd it must sound to these people. But they listened in silence. "She said we must kill every one of them."

"I have some sympathy with that," Jack said.

The ground shook beneath them, and a loose piece of glass fell from one of the broken windows.

"The tremors are becoming more frequent," Ruth said. "And this isn't a seismically active area."

"There's something in the lake," Jack said. "We need to find out what it is."

"Carry out any surveillance you need around the lake or in the southern part, near the larger island, but keep away from the smaller island," Superintendent Dale said. "I hope to initiate negotiations with the terrorists."

"Do they want to negotiate?" Jack asked.

"We'll see," Superintendent Dale said.

As the meeting ended, Luke had mixed feelings. He wanted the negotiations to succeed, but he'd also have been happy with a military rescue, providing it worked. The sooner he got Molly back, the better.

Superintendent Dale and his colleagues from the Counter Terrorism Unit had created a makeshift office on a large desk that faced the only unbroken window in the room. Luke stood nearby, unsure what to do but ready to offer any assistance if needed. Ruth Hardy had already taken the lobster into the field laboratory she'd set up on the table in what looked like a secret section of the library. The special forces occupied the wooden table in the middle of the main room, and two marines worked on their laptops. Luke looked out of the window.

An old-fashioned telephone on the desk rang. Dale picked up the receiver, pressing the loudspeaker button at the same time.

"My name is Frank Olney."

The man spoke English with an accent and formed his words in the same way they'd been misspelled in the language learning notebook he'd found at Battersea.

"My name's Superintendent Dale." He spoke with a calm and reassuring voice. It was part of the negotiator's act—a way to build trust and rapport. Luke had once written a booklet advising the police on how to negotiate. "I'm happy to talk about any problems you have."

"I have two demands," Olney said. "First I want the removal of all forces from the lake. Second, I want compensation for the destruction of my property in south London."

"The military are here for our protection," Dale said. "They came because you attacked us. If I may ask, what did attack us?"

"Those are our special forces. But if you follow my instructions, you'll have nothing to fear," Olney said.

The man spoke so calmly and sounded so reasonable that Luke had to remind himself of all that had happened.

"The property in Battersea was rented. The landlord has lost money, not you. Can you explain what loss you're speaking of?"

"Very special equipment."

"What sort of equipment?" Dale asked. "We need to know this in order to estimate its value."

"Ten million would be a good start."

"That's a lot of money," Dale said.

"Which your government has," Olney said. "We need the money transferred to an account of our choosing."

The man sounded bored as he spoke, not like someone would if they cared about what they were saying.

"The price of not complying is the death of the hostages."

"How many do you have?"

"Nine."

"May I ask who?"

"We'll send you the names later. We're holding your inspector."

"May we speak with Inspector Gully?"

There was a delay of several seconds. The background sound altered. The man was in a room.

"Inspector Gully here."

"Inspector, how are you?" Superintendent Dale asked.

"Cold, but I've been treated well so far."

Luke leant forward. Someone was talking in the background.

But Superintendent Dale spoke again. "Have you seen—"

Frank Olney interrupted the superintendent. "That's enough, Superintendent Dale. Now you know he's alive."

"I need to know that the other hostages are alive, too."

"Remove your forces from the lake." There was an underlying threat to his words that hadn't been there before that worried Luke. The line went dead.

"That's not an option," Captain Willis told Superintendent Dale.

The superintendent nodded.

"He's not negotiating seriously; he's playing for time," Luke said.

Willis glanced at Luke. "I agree with Dr Lee. It rings false."

"Can you play back the recording?" Luke asked. "Someone was talking in the background while Gully was speaking."

They played back the recording. It was Olney. Luke replayed the audio multiple times, and Superintendent Dale returned to his team. It sounded familiar to Luke. Numbers and telling the time had been one of the classes in the notebook, and Amelia had translated numbers, too.

"They said something about the early morning," Luke said.

Superintendent Dale raised an eyebrow. "What exactly?" he asked.

Luke shrugged. "That something important will happen. Leander Amis said the same."

"Perhaps we should go to the island and ask them," Jack said.

"You've really bought into this idea of something bad happening tomorrow morning," the superintendent said, "but we don't know that."

"No, but everything points to it," Luke said. "Amis's letter to me mentioned a possible atrocity to be committed at sunrise on Sunday. Amelia Blake's experiences seem to confirm this."

"The visions of a psychic don't prove anything," Dale said.

Some of Dale's staff grinned, but Luke noticed that no one else did. They were too focussed on finding solutions to think of anything else.

A shout came from outside. Jack was through the french windows in seconds, Captain Willis and Superintendent Dale were right behind him. Luke followed them onto the muddy lawn. A lizard stood in the shallow water. It bit into the neck of a commando and dropped his body in the mud. Then it took the man's assault rifle, held it in the air, and screeched. Turning, it ran straight into the water. Two commandos fired, but it seemed to make little difference. The creature dived under the water and was gone.

"Keep everyone away from the edge of the mere," Willis ordered a corporal.

They re-entered the library, and the captain addressed Dale. "This is not a normal hostage negotiation. It's time we upped the game."

"No hostage negotiation is normal," Dale said. The telephone rang, and he picked it up.

"That was a lesson. The next lesson will follow shortly, if you don't comply," Olney said.

"We're ready to listen to your concerns," Superintendent Dale said smoothly. "Talk to us about the hostages."

"What do you want to know?"

Luke snatched the receiver from Dale. He no longer cared about courtesy or that he was still under arrest; he needed to know more.

"How do we know the hostages are alive?"

## 24

Molly stood shivering in front of her, and Amelia quickly searched for anything that could be used for clothing. There wasn't much, but Molly needed to get out of her soaked clothes immediately. Amelia stripped the bed of its meagre bedding and used the nail in the wall to rip it in two as Molly started undressing the baby. Once the baby was out of the wet clothes, Amelia wrapped him in one half of the bedding.

"Where were they holding you?" Amelia asked as Molly took off her wet clothes.

"In the lake."

Amelia thought she'd misunderstood. "On the other island?"

"No, at the bottom of the lake."

Amelia looked up, surprised.

"They live there," Molly said. Amelia passed her the other half of the bedding, which she wrapped around her. "There are other women there. Most of them are pregnant." Shivering, she kicked the wet pile of clothes away, and Amelia gave Molly her coat.

"How many?" Amelia asked.

"Six of us. And one man who they keep separate. They treat us like farm animals. I had to escape."

"Of course." Amelia wasn't sure what to say. "But they caught you again."

"When I got close to the island. I should've swum to the shore."

Amelia shook her head. "It's too far."

The baby cried, and Molly began breastfeeding him. "We're like cows; they milk us."

"What do you mean?" Amelia asked, feeling disturbed by the series of strange images coming to her mind.

"Not literally. I mean they take our blood."

Amelia felt sick, but she had to know more. "How much?"

"A cup or two."

"How do you feel after?"

"Tired."

Amelia guessed they were taking more than blood.

"Who are you?" Molly asked.

"My name's Amelia Blake. I've been working with Luke Lee. We've been trying to find you." Molly's eyes opened wide. "Yes, your husband."

"Is he here?"

"I don't know." She told Molly everything she knew, from her meeting with Luke to her kidnapping.

"How badly was he shot?" Molly asked.

"It's a surface wound. He'll be okay."

Molly relaxed a little but still asked several more questions about Luke, which Amelia answered as well as she could. "I'm a nurse, and I've seen a lot of head wounds. It was superficial, but he'll need a couple of stitches."

Hoping to change the conversation, Amelia asked Molly

about her abduction. Apparently, just as Amelia had been, Molly had been semi-conscious in the van and hardly remembered the first part of the journey. But she described the structure under the mere in detail.

"It's made of metal. And it's without windows. At least, I didn't see any."

"Did you swim from the bottom?"

"No, they have pods. I'd seen them used before. As soon as I had a chance, I sneaked inside and pulled levers. It made a lot of noise, and the guards rushed at me, but the door closed, and I rose quickly. It was dark, and I couldn't see anything, but I saw through a small window that I'd reached the surface, so I decided to swim, but one of them caught me, and here I am."

"Where are they from?" Amelia asked.

"I've got no idea; they're not exactly chatty. And they speak a strange language. Definitely not from this country."

"Why are they there?" Amelia asked. "I mean, why would they build something under the mere?"

"When one woman asked, they beat her unconscious. No one asked again." She paused and looked around the cold stone room. "I'm a bit closer to Luke, at least. Is there any way to escape?"

"I was hoping to climb through the window, but I'd probably slip to my death. A better way may appear later."

Voices came from outside the room. "That's Frank Olney," Molly whispered.

"The leader?"

Molly started to shake her head, then seemed to change her mind. "One of them."

The door opened and Olney walked inside. He was about six foot one and had a chiselled, angular-looking face. Amelia reflexively moved back. He glanced at her wrists.

Then, moving fast, he grabbed her by her hair. She screamed as he pulled her behind him. She pressed down on his hand to stop her hair from ripping out. Letting go, he shoved her against the wall.

Angel stood in the open doorway.

"Out!" Olney said.

Angel slammed the door shut. Olney's voice vibrated sending a chill up Amelia's spine. He had magical training and projected it when he spoke. She knew something about this skill but had never witnessed it used so effectively before.

Olney watched Amelia for a few seconds. "I have questions for you." Then he glanced at Molly. "I'll speak to you later."

Turning his attention back to Amelia, he took hold of her wrists, which stung when he gripped them tightly. She started to feel dizzy, as if some pressure pushed against her mind.

"Relax. It'll hurt less," Olney said.

Amelia resisted, but he was physically stronger. And psychically stronger, too. Something like a psychic punch hit her, and her legs turned to jelly. She slid down the damp tower wall until she sat on the floor. She shivered as he entered her mind, and again she had the feeling of falling backwards. She saw bright lights, and her dizziness threatened to engulf her. She retreated deeper inside her mind, and he followed, eventually catching her and pinning her like a living butterfly in a cabinet.

He moved adeptly through her thoughts; she sensed that this was not the first time he'd invaded another person's mind. Her memories flashed before her one by one. Olney was sifting through her thoughts and experiences. She heard herself discussing the enemy with Luke, and she felt his attention focus for several seconds on what little she knew of his language.

He continued his search.

She saw herself inside the Akashic Library. Olney was now paying close attention to her every memory of the incident. He paused over her search for the witch. Then he jumped to the summoning of the witch. She sensed his shock, and he frantically searched for something. He tugged at her memories, but they were no longer there. She couldn't remember anything the witch had said. The man pulled himself from her mind and stepped back. He was breathing heavily.

"What have you done?" His face was pale.

She wasn't sure; she sensed she must have done something right, but her headache was distracting her. And she felt nauseous. Her mind felt strangely blank, as if there was something she should remember but couldn't, and she hoped that whatever he'd done hadn't damaged her brain.

"You foolish woman," Olney said. "You've interfered in things you don't understand."

Amelia felt numb, as if she'd drunk a strange cocktail that had gone straight to her head. One that gave you a hangover before you'd finished the glass. She heard the door slam.

"Amelia, are you alright?" Molly said, helping her to her feet.

Amelia staggered towards the bed and sat down. She felt nauseous and had a terrible headache.

"Never felt better."

Molly grinned, but when she looked into Amelia's eyes, her face became serious. "What just happened?"

"He went inside my head. My brain feels fuzzy." Amelia gasped, trying not to pass out.

"Amelia!" Molly held her hands. "You're making me nervous."

Some memories returned. "He sensed something in my mind but couldn't find it."

"What?"

Amelia remembered the thought—the thing he'd searched for. She put her finger to her lips, suddenly realising that she was trembling.

"What is it?" Molly said.

Amelia shook her head. "I can't tell you. If he heard, he'd kill me."

## 25

"Luke?"

"Molly!" Luke pressed the old telephone receiver to his ear so hard it hurt.

"I'm in the tower." She spoke quickly. "I'm okay. Our son's well—"

"Your proof," a man said. He spoke with authority. It was no longer Frank Olney speaking.

"Follow our instructions. Remove the military from the lake."

Superintendent Dale pulled the phone away from Luke, but the man's voice retained its velvety smoothness. "That's difficult. You must understand that. I'm sure you know there are rules we must follow, and—"

A gunshot interrupted him, and Luke started.

"Molly Lee is dead," the man said. A child cried in the background. The man put the phone down.

"I'm sorry," Superintendent Dale said to Luke as he hung up.

"No!"

Luke fell to his knees, hardly noticing the broken glass.

Vaguely, he felt hands supporting him. They helped him to a chair, and he sat heavily; he hardly heard what people were saying. Jack and Ruth remained with him. The rest of the room had returned to their own tasks. He breathed deeply; he was someone who had always avoided emotional scenes, but he was struggling now.

"You can't be sure," Jack said.

"I heard the shot," Luke said numbly.

He stared blankly around the room. If Molly was gone . . . He didn't want to think about that.

"Your child is still alive," Ruth said. "He needs you."

She was right. For his son's sake he needed to think clearly. Luke felt some of his life return. He'd find his son, and he'd do whatever he could to fight these evil men.

A flurry of orange snow gusted through one of the broken windows, and Luke spat out some that had blown into his mouth. The carpet was so dirty that it hardly mattered.

"This is more sand than snow," Jack said, wiping his mouth with the back of his hand.

They stood in silence for a few seconds and then Ruth spoke.

"The lobster's much stranger than I first thought."

They followed her to her field laboratory in the hidden library. A rugged-looking microscope sitting on three rubber-coated legs was at the far end of the table, and the box with the lobster was in the middle.

"Look." She pointed at the lobster.

Luke and Jack stared at the lobster for a few moments and then shared a glance.

"Well?" Ruth asked.

"What are we looking at?" Jack asked.

In exasperation, Ruth pointed again. "Its eyes."

Luke hardly cared about the lobster, but he forced himself to look. He couldn't see anything unusual either.

"Ruth, we're not zoologists," Jack said.

"Step back."

They did, and seconds later, two eyes peered at them over the top of the box. Ruth moved her hand, and the eyes followed.

"It has twelve-inch extendable eye stalks!"

"What does this mean?" Jack asked.

"It means it's unique. There's nothing like it in the world. And look at the silver rings along the stalk. This lobster is very old."

Luke watched the lobster watching him. "It is strange." She wasn't joking.

"Perhaps you've discovered a new species," Jack said.

"Luke discovered it," Ruth said. "This lobster is the biggest creature we've found, but the number of microscopic ones is huge, and they're pretty weird, too. I'm also worried that exposure to these strange things may be exposing us to illness."

"What kind?" Luke asked. He'd decided to learn anything he could that might help him rescue his son.

"The sickness that spread through south London seems to have almost disappeared. We think the skin rashes, nausea, and loss of smell are caused by exposure to the orange snow. But I'm concerned that something in it may also be causing hallucinations. Some of the men have been acting strangely. Inspector Gully was acting strangely before he was taken, and some men have complained of seeing things or hearing voices."

"I've had visions," Jack said. They all turned to look at him.

"What did you see?" Luke asked.

"Amelia Blake. She called me from the tower. And I saw flames."

"I thought I heard Amelia's voice, too," Luke said.

"Anything else?" Ruth asked.

Luke shook his head. "Even if something in the snow caused hallucinations, what are the chances it would cause similar hallucinations?"

She shook her head. "I've never heard of a hallucinogen acting like that. But it could be possible if the people suffering from it were sharing a similar experience."

Luke thought she didn't look convinced of this herself.

Another tremor shook the manor.

"Captain?" one of the marines working on the wooden table in the main part of the library said. "You might want to see this."

The four of them joined Willis at the table and crowded round the man's laptop. A sonar screen showed an image of a large structure at the bottom of the lake. Four smaller objects moved close to the bottom and then disappeared.

"What was that?" Ruth asked.

Captain Willis shook his head. "I don't know, but something's down there, alright. It's big, too."

"Things are moving beside it," the marine said. "But whatever they are, they just vanished."

"What are they?" Ruth asked.

Luke already knew. "The lizards are going home."

Jack nodded.

"One more thing," the marine said. "The epicentre of the tremors is at the bottom of the lake."

The telephone rang again, and the same man spoke over the loudspeaker. "You've been flying your helicopter around the lake; I presume you've found nothing of interest. Now it's time for you to leave."

"I'm Superintendent Dale, the police negotiator. We have no further plans to fly over the mere."

"This is an improvement."

Superintendent Dale spoke again. "Would it be unreasonable for me to ask your name?"

"Not unreasonable."

The man on the island spoke in accented English. Luke listened carefully to his accent, but he still had no idea of where he was from. The voice was almost charming. Luke had to force himself to remember that this man, or one of his accomplices, had murdered his wife.

"I am Nimori."

"Is that a first name?" Dale asked.

"Nick Nimori."

While one of the police constables checked for the name, Luke thought about the man they were dealing with. The methods for detecting a liar were fine in theory, when you could ask questions freely and establish a baseline that gives an understanding of how a person speaks and reacts in normal situations, but in this situation it was almost impossible. And the man was so controlled. Superintendent Dale had been doing little more than restate Nimori's demands and confirm that he understood. It was an attempt to gain the man's trust, which wasn't working in Luke's opinion.

"You do understand," Dale said, "that I can't order the removal of the military. But I can assure you that you'll be treated with respect and dignity."

"You must try to do as I say."

"I'm sure you want nothing but complete honesty from me," Dale said calmly. His voice had changed to an emphatic downward intonation to stress an unalterable fact. Another technique. "You must understand that we're not permitted to just leave, but I can assure you of fair treatment," Dale said.

Luke became alert as the man switched into his language. There seemed to be someone else with him. Olney perhaps. Luke's brow was furrowed as he concentrated.

"They mentioned time again," he said quietly.

"Could you tell us more about what you want from us?" Superintendent Dale asked. "And what is your time frame?"

"Let's compromise," Nimori said.

"We can talk about that," Dale answered.

"The police may remain but move your military away from the edges of the lake, and we can talk about a possible surrender."

Superintendent Dale glanced at the others. "I'll speak with the chief military officer. It may take a few hours to move them back."

"We can speak later," Nimori said.

Jack leant forward. "What's in the lake?"

There was a moment's silence before Nimori spoke. "Water?"

"We've seen it," Jack said.

"If you mean our experimental station, we can show you around it later, depending on the success of the negotiations."

The phone went dead. Superintendent Dale answered his mobile phone. The room went quiet as he listened and then explained the situation. "Yes, sir." He put the phone away. "Whitehall has sent us new instructions. We're not to attack. We must continue to negotiate," Dale said. "It looks like we're finally making progress. I suggest a partial withdrawal of military forces. Perhaps to the road near the manor. We could replace the marines surrounding the mere by police."

"That didn't work very well last time," Captain Willis said.

"The situation's changed," Dale said. "We've been instructed to learn more about the structure beneath the lake. If they're willing to surrender, this could save lives."

"How do we know they're negotiating in good faith?" Luke asked.

"We don't," Dale said. "But unless we attempt to negotiate, we'll never find out."

"Amis believed something catastrophic would happen at sunrise," Luke said.

Jack nodded. "They're up to something."

Captain Willis received a call. His face darkened, but he nodded. Looking up at the others, he spoke. "Negotiations are to take precedence over any military action. I've been ordered only to launch a rescue mission if the negotiations totally breakdown."

Superintendent Dale nodded. "That is so. Now let me do my job. And Dr Lee, you may continue to provide interpretation, but keep it to linguistics."

"We need to understand what's under the mere," Jack said.

"We will," Superintendent Dale said. "It'll come from negotiation followed by a search, not military action."

"Jack!" Ruth said.

He stormed out of the library and into the garden.

"Let him go," Willis said.

But Ruth wasn't listening, and she went after him, and Luke, feeling the need to get away from the atmosphere in the library, followed, too.

"Where did he go?" Luke asked.

Ruth searched the shore. Then she pointed at the row of black canoes. "Jack, no!"

Luke stared in disbelief as Jack climbed into one of the canoes. A marine sergeant shouted, but Jack was already slipping through the water in the stolen canoe.

"I feel sick," Ruth said. "His career's over."

Captain Willis ran along the shore. "Jack Ross. Return immediately!"

But Jack continued to paddle into the fog.

"You're finished!" Willis shouted.

But Jack had disappeared from sight.

"He's taken a Glock," the sergeant said.

The captain softly shook his head. "I hope it's worth the sacrifice."

"He may find your son," Ruth said quietly to Luke.

Luke felt a sudden surge of warmth towards Jack and wished he was fighting beside him.

## 26

Jack paddled through the fog. He could have moved faster, but he wanted to be invisible. It was possible the lizards had senses he wasn't aware of—perhaps they could detect changes of pressure in the water.

He knew he'd lost his job, but some things were more important. And he knew there were lives to save on the island. He had no regrets.

The black canoe was basic—an ancient design coming from Inuit kayaks—constructed from wood and fabric. Nothing fancy, yet these boats were some of the best in the world at what they did. And his squadron was the best. He didn't care about battle-bred reptiles. The squadron's motto was by strength and guile; he'd live or die by it today.

He had his radio, which was turned off, his knife, and the Glock. The pistol might not stop one of these things, but well-aimed shots would slow one down. He'd have preferred an assault rifle, but stealing one would have been too difficult. If all he achieved was to locate the hostages, then he could increase the chances of their survival once the country's leaders came to their senses and ordered a rescue operation. But he wanted more than that. He wanted to defend his country against this evil force.

Jack stopped paddling.

Something was moving under the water, and he pulled out his pistol. He couldn't see anything, but he knew it was there. Gut feelings had saved his life several times, and he seldom ignored them, and when he did, he always regretted it. The boat bobbed up and down as small waves washed around him, and he wondered why operations like this always seemed to happen in extremely cold places. Then the feeling that something was moving beneath him disappeared, and he resumed paddling. It didn't matter how long he took to reach the island. What mattered was reaching it.

As he moved through the darkness, he was aware of the water lapping around him, and the rhythm of his paddling. His mind was momentarily freed. Gliding through the cold, dark night, he felt as if he were one small part of something larger—that forces greater than him were directing his life. Whatever evil lurked in the tower or under the dark mere, he was an agent of its destruction. He was sure of that.

He was also sure the feelings he'd had, and the faint images he'd imagined, had originated from Amelia Blake. But how she'd made that happen, he had no idea. Perhaps she wasn't consciously doing anything at all. Perhaps he was just picking up her distress. But this wasn't the first time in his life things like this had happened. Once, a friend had gone missing in action. Jack had pictured him lying in a ravine and had known exactly where to find him. When questioned, he'd told the truth, but no one had believed him.

A cold wind blew over the mere, and Jack shivered. He could now see the island looming out of the darkness, and he swung his canoe to the right, wanting to circle around to the far side, hopefully away from any eyes that might be watching. He thought about the attacks on his country as he rounded the island. He agreed with the general consensus that a foreign power must have built the underwater structure. It made sense that the lizards were bred there, too. Advanced genetic engineering was clearly the most logical explanation. But he couldn't understand the threat. What would happen at sunrise? It was still over three hours away. What could a foreign power gain from causing chaos in his country? And in such a remote area. Then there were the things Ruth was discovering almost every day. It was too much to think about. He hoped to learn more on the island.

His attention was brought back to the boat when he entered choppy water. Ten more minutes of paddling, and he'd reached the far side of the island. Despite the full moon, he was mostly invisible apart from his face. He wished he'd had the chance to blacken it, but that would have alerted the men. Instead, he pulled his woollen hat down over his ears and put his collar up. At least the canoe was black, making it almost invisible to the naked eye. He moved closer.

Five minutes later, he was in position, floating about thirty yards from the island. He waited and watched. The tower was visible through the fog because of the full moon, and a faint light was coming from one of the upper floors. A screech and a splash came from the island. Reptiles were in the water. He waited. Thirty minutes passed before he paddled silently towards the shore. The only sound was the wind on the water.

When he was about fifteen yards from the island, a figure moved along its shoreline. He paddled slowly. The figure was human, making him easier to kill than a lizard. But he turned and paced back the way he'd come. Something had caught his attention. Jack was now five yards from the shore, surrounded by tall reeds. Easing himself out of the canoe, he gritted his teeth when he slipped into the frigid water. He was unsure how deep it was, and he sank to his thighs before his feet touched the bottom. Crouching by the partially hidden canoe, he waited, and eventually the man moved away.

As Jack waded through the brackish water, something gripped his leg. He forced himself to move with a calmness he didn't feel as it tugged at him more strongly. Stifling a shout, he pulled himself onto the shore as its grip tightened further.

Turning round, he pointed his pistol at the dark shape clutching his leg.

## 27

Moonlight shone on his leg, and Jack only just stopped himself from shooting. Slowly his breathing returned to normal, and taking out his knife, he cut through the clump of weeds clinging to his legs and dropped them back into the lake. He watched the ripples in the dark water for several seconds, but nothing emerged. Turning, he studied the tower, and his stomach sank when he realised that there were no ground-floor doors or windows, nor was there any cover apart from the fog. Not on this side. He waited, watching for any sign of life.

Something splashed in the water about twenty yards to his right, and Jack strained to see through a new wave of fog rolling in from the mere. A head emerged and its frills extended, then flattened against its neck. The lizard waded ashore, dragging something through the reeds. Jack dropped as low as he could and waited. Two more lizards bounded through the fog, while the first one continued to pull something from the water. Then he recognised it. The lizard pulled the body of a dead companion. Something must have happened, or perhaps it was from the earlier conflict. One less was good for him.

The lizards stood together. It was almost as if they were speaking. He could hear their hisses and muted screeches from where he hid. One of the lizards pointed a crooked claw to the upper part of the tower. Jack looked up. He made out the shapes of two figures looking down from an upper window. One of them reached out, grasping the stone wall. Without warning, a lizard rushed towards the tower, and hardly slowing at all, it ran straight up the outer wall towards the window. The figures appeared to freeze as it closed in on them. Then it scooped one of them from the window. The figure cried out; it was a woman. Jack guessed they must be the hostages. He watched as the lizard then pulled the other woman out and ran up the wall. It disappeared over the turrets, taking the women with it. The remaining pair of giant lizards resumed their patrol around the island. He strained to see what they were carrying.

"Impossible," Jack whispered to himself as they came closer.

The moonlight and shadows must be playing tricks with his eyes. He blinked and looked again. This time, they were even closer, and there was no doubt. Each one carried a heavy machine gun as easily if they were regular submachine guns. They looked natural, too. If they hadn't been giant reptiles, he'd have assumed they were commandos from the way they carried their weapons.

A movement to his left caught his attention and that of the reptiles. One of the men was walking towards them; he had an assault rifle swung over his shoulder. It seemed the man and creatures had divided the shore into patrol sections. The man waved at the lizards, and they returned the signal. Jack prayed they wouldn't check the reed bed where he hid. Resisting the urge to back away as the lizards approached, Jack remained motionless. They walked past him, continuing their patrol.

When he judged them far enough away, Jack ran to the tower, crouched low. He was a competent rock climber, and he hoped that this old tower, with the combination of stones, rocks, bricks, and spaces that formed its walls, would make climbing relatively easy. Unless it collapsed on him. The fog blowing in from the lake was now his friend, and he climbed quickly, mostly concerned about stones falling to the ground and attracting attention. He paused again when the reptiles returned. It seemed that each pair patrolled a particular stretch of shoreline.

One of them hissed, and the other replied in a complex series of hisses and clicks. But amongst those strange sounds he heard human words. He might not be a linguist like the professor, but he recognised a language when he heard one. He clung to the outer wall in silence. It was obvious the lizards were intelligent.

When they'd disappeared from view, he pulled himself up to the window, aware that for a few seconds he'd be vulnerable as he climbed inside. Pausing, his body half on the thick ledge of the glassless window, he listened. Although not patient by nature, Jack had learnt patience in the military. He'd had jobs that combined incredible degrees of boredom and danger, and so hanging on the wall while he listened was something he did without thinking.

When he'd heard no sound for two minutes, he pulled himself into the hole. It was one large room. A single candle burnt on a table in the centre of the room, sending flickering shadows into the dark corners. Next to the candle, a pistol protruded from a backpack. This meant someone was close. He waited for another two minutes but heard nothing. Jack squeezed through the window and gently dropped to the ground, but his pistol caught on a nail as he fell, clattering across the floor.

A figure stepped from the shadows.

## 28

"Hello, Jack," Angel said. A blade was in his hand.

Despite the cold, Jack was sweating. He was more nervous than he liked. But controlled fear kept him sharp.

"I should have killed you a long time ago." He pulled out his knife

"What about the rules?" Angel asked.

"Like the rules in the mountains?"

"Get off your high horse, Jack," Angel snapped. He edged towards the pistol on the table. "You know it's a job. And you're a government killer, just like I was." Angel glanced at the table, and Jack studied his eyes. For once he wasn't on drugs. "You know they deserved it."

"They were prisoners."

Jack prepared for the inevitable rush for the weapon on the wooden table; his own pistol was too far away.

"You murdered Bonnie," Jack said.

"She worked for the Security Service, and if she hadn't struggled so hard, she'd still be alive. We're no different, whatever you think."

Jack didn't believe him but didn't reply.

They ran at the table, reaching it at the same time, but Jack hit the table harder, knocking it into Angel; the pistol slid across the floor. Angel grabbed the table and slammed it into his hand, sending the knife clattering to the floor. Grabbing the table legs, Jack used it as a battering ram and pinned Angel to the wall. Jack punched him in the head several times until he dropped his blade, but Angel managed to push the table away and attempt a takedown.

Falling awkwardly to the floor, Jack felt a pain in his leg, but he continued to fight. He'd been one of the best grapplers in his unit, and he felt he had an advantage on the ground, but it was still hard. He slowly worked his way into a better position. After almost a minute, he flipped the man over, and from the upper position, he punched hard, repeatedly. Despite a broken nose, Angel kept fighting and kept taking the punishment. Jack was beginning to tire, but he'd pushed through exhaustion before. Angel finally stopped struggling and lay on the stone floor, but his eyelids flickered open.

"You were lucky, Jack," Angel said as blood flowed from his mouth. Then he passed out.

Jack's face was flushed, and all he could hear was a pounding in his ears. Shakily pushing himself away from the prone man, he stood up. He'd pulled a muscle in his leg. A roar sent him stumbling backwards into the wall. The panther leapt from the window, fire falling from its mouth. It walked to Angel and sniffed him.

He couldn't fight the thing unarmed, especially not after the fight he'd just had. Jack looked at the pistols lying near the walls. The panther seemed to notice and snarled. Then it pawed Angel. It looked like a dog pawing its master. Bending down, it closed its jaws around the front of Angel's jacket and dragged him backwards towards the stairs where it adjusted its grip. It half lifted him in its mouth, gripping his upper arm and shoulder. Then it pulled him down the circular stairs.

Jack limped across the room and picked up his knife and both pistols. A set of stairs ran up and down the outer wall. Jack was aware that there may be a lizard on the roof, but he had no choice but to go up. He started climbing the stairs but moved slowly feeling an acute pain in his chest, he suspected he'd bruised his ribs. He rested for a few minutes until his breathing returned to normal but started moving again when he heard movement below. Seconds could mean the difference between life and death. He climbed faster in spite of the pain.

"You," a man said.

Jack turned to see Olney and another man, probably Nick Nimori, wearing decorated robes and conical hats— some sort of ceremonial costume. They also carried automatic weapons. He climbed faster. The third floor had a trapdoor over the stairs. He climbed through and slammed it shut behind him. Luckily there was an old bolt, which he rammed into place. He heard the men running up the stone steps beneath him. A small lamp hung from the wall, and like the lower floors, it was one large room. He continued up the stairs. The fourth floor was divided into smaller rooms. All had padlocks on the outside. Shots came from below.

Breathing heavily, he climbed the final flight of stairs. The stairs ended suddenly, and a trapdoor blocked his way. He pulled back the bolt, but it seemed to be locked on the other side, too. He knocked it with the butt of his pistol.

"Open up! I'm Jack Ross. I'm working with the police." *Or was. And probably ex-MI5 by now,* he thought.

He heard stones being rolled from the trapdoor. Then it

opened. Amelia Blake and a woman with a baby strapped to her back peered down at him. He climbed through to the roof and slammed it shut again, and then slammed a rusty metal bolt into place. It wouldn't last long against any serious effort to break it open, but it was all there was. The two women rolled the half-dozen rocks and stones back onto the top of the door.

"I'm Amelia Blake."

"I know. Your friend Luke Lee is on the shore."

"Luke's here?" the other woman said.

"This is Molly Lee, his wife," Amelia said.

"Luke thinks you're dead."

"The gunshot?"

Jack nodded, then looked around. The light of the full moon illuminated the top of the tower.

"It's gone," Amelia said.

He knew she was talking about the lizard.

"Will that hold them?" Molly asked, waving toward the rocks on the trapdoor.

"It might slow them. Where did the lizard go?"

"It ran down the side of the tower," Amelia said.

"Where are the other hostages?" Jack asked.

"Under the lake," Molly said.

That was what he'd suspected.

"And someone may be on another floor of the tower," Amelia said. "I heard some sounds."

Jack took out his radio and contacted base. He gave them a very shortened version of what had happened, then said, "We need a helicopter, now!"

"There's one on the way," Captain Willis said. "Are you fit to use ropes?"

"I have to be."

Someone banged on the trapdoor.

Jack limped to the ramparts, searching through the dark fog for approaching helicopter. Amelia and Molly, holding her child, joined him.

"There!" Molly said as the helicopter pattered through the fog towards them.

Then he looked over the side of the tower. "Not good!"

"What?" Amelia asked. She looked over and fell back into Molly.

A lizard ran towards him with a heavy machine gun in one arm. It aimed at the helicopter. Jack fired his pistol repeatedly, and it fell back a few feet before regaining its footing. Then it fired at him. The Wildcat swept round, and the door gunner opened fire, cutting into the lizard—the lizard's gun dropped to the ground. But it didn't die and continued crawling towards him. When it saw him watching, it spat. It was fast, and he only just dodged the acidic spittle, which sizzled on the moss-covered parapet.

The helicopter made another pass. This time the gunner cut the lizard in half.

"Yes," Jack said, looking over the edge.

"They're hard to kill," Molly said.

"You're not joking." Jack waved to the helicopter, and it moved towards them.

He holstered his empty pistol and checked Angel's. It was nearly out of ammo, too. He cursed again; the trapdoor was starting to fragment.

He turned on the radio. "Get us out of here!"

The helicopter gunner nodded. With the pattering rotor blades, Jack couldn't hear the reply.

"Jack—" Molly said.

Splinters of wood came from the trapdoor. They were shooting their way through.

"There's another one crawling up the wall. It's carrying a machine gun."

Jack was unsure which would kill them first—the eight-foot lizard on the wall or the killers coming through the trapdoor.

Molly and Amelia stood close to him.

"I've only got two rounds left. I'll shoot the first thing that attacks us," Jack said.

"Jack!" Amelia said. "There's more of them!"

More of the things were crawling quickly up the outside of the tower as the helicopter moved into position above them. He counted three in total.

"We need help now!" Jack shouted over the radio. "I've got three monsters with heavy machine guns, crawling up the tower, and two psychopaths with assault rifles, who think they're magicians, trying to kill us!"

Then the trapdoor exploded in a shower of splinters, and two magicians with ceremonial robes and guns stepped onto the roof.

## 29

"Molly!" Luke shouted in surprise.

Jack had been right; he'd been too quick to assume the worst. The noise of the helicopter blades prevented her from hearing, but she looked up. A weight lifted from him. He continued to watch the scene beneath him from the helicopter he'd argued his way onto, swearing he might be needed for urgent translation. In part, they'd agreed in order to shut him up. And in return, he'd agreed not to interfere, but now, to the gunner's annoyance, he clung to a rail by the open space as he looked down.

His worry returned when two heavily armed men in ceremonial robes rushed onto the roof. Then the lizards climbing the tower walls opened fire with heavy machine guns. The pilot swerved away from the tower. Luke moved away from the open space to one of the windows where he watched the lizards crawling over the turrets, and the men facing Molly and his son. He had a feeling of despair. This wasn't going as planned. The Wildcat swept down, and the gunner fired at the nearest two lizards. They instantly returned fire, shattering the cockpit window and hitting the copilot. The pilot swerved away again.

One of the men pointed a gun at Molly. Another made a cutting gesture across his throat. It was over. Three lizards were now on the roof watching the helicopter. Nimori spoke to one of them. Luke had heard Jack's report on speaking lizards.

"We have to turn back," the pilot said.

Luke reluctantly agreed. He didn't want to risk the lives of Molly, his son, or his friends. And the copilot needed urgent medical attention. But the helicopter suddenly lurched to one side. The gunner shouted and tried to adjust his aim. When the helicopter swayed again, Luke leant through the open door and looked down. A lizard hung on the rope ladder. The pilot swung the helicopter away, but the thing climbed up adeptly, and although the gunner tried to point his gun directly down, the angle was too sharp. The lizard swung wildly beneath the helicopter, disappearing from view. The pilot was rocking the helicopter from side to side, trying to get rid of the creature, and veering too low over the island, its blades only just missing the tower.

For a few seconds, Luke could see Molly's face clearly. She looked up at him but stepped back when a lizard moved towards her. The lizard grabbed her and pulled her across the roof. He chilled when it dragged his wife and son over the turrets. He was losing her a second time, and there was nothing he could do.

A loud scratching turned his attention to the inside of the helicopter. A clawed hand reached inside and gutted the gunner. The man screamed as it flung him out of the cabin. Luke hated the monsters, and he crawled slowly towards the machine gun but was thrown back when the helicopter lurched again. The lizard started to crawl into the helicopter, its acrid smell filling the cabin. The pilot cried out. Then Luke was thrown forwards as the helicopter shifted again, and he grabbed hold of the machine gun. The lizard's frills opened wide. It opened its mouth, preparing to spit, but his finger was already moving around the trigger. He pulled it, and the creature squealed as it flew through the air. Almost falling through the open doorway himself, he gripped a rail by the door and stared down at the tower. A lizard climbed down the side with Molly in its arms.

Then the helicopter started spinning, and Luke turned to the pilot. He was moaning and clutching his face. The lizard's acid had destroyed it. The co-pilot was already dead. They were going down. Like a spinning brick, the helicopter careered towards the lake. Luke lost his grip just before impact and flew through the open doorway. The shock of the frigid water was like receiving a hard punch. He surfaced as the helicopter sank and swam towards the island. He was only about twenty yards from the shore, but the coldness slowed him. The thought of Molly and his child kept him going. Staggering onto the shore, he knew that whatever happened, he couldn't stop moving, otherwise, he'd freeze to death. And there was a chance Molly was still on the island. Behind him, a small inflatable craft was circling the area where the helicopter had gone down. Other inflatables raced towards the island.

Ruth was in one of the boats.

The boat moved fast towards him. It looked like he was going to be rescued, but he had to find Molly first. Then Ruth pointed at something behind him. Turning, he saw the lizard standing at the base of the tower watching them. Molly moved in its arms.

He ran towards it.

"Molly!"

Paying no attention to her shouts to keep away, he kept running. Perhaps the cold, or perhaps desperation, had distorted his reasoning. He knew he couldn't kill it, but he had to do something. The lizard watched the approaching boats, and, without a glance, it swatted him away and ran straight to the lake, taking Molly with it. He chased it, but the thing was quick, and he could hardly even think straight, he was shaking so much from the cold.

Ruth jumped out of the boat and ran along the shore directly towards it. One of the commandoes was with her. The man pointed his pistol at the thing.

"No."

But Luke was so chilled he could only croak. He was terrified the man would hit Molly or the baby, but his shot was good, hitting the lizard in its leg, yet it did no more than slow it. It used Molly as a shield. She was frantically struggling when it turned and strode deeper into the lake. His vision was starting to fade, but he was determined not to faint. He watched his wife and child disappear under the dark water.

Seeing something floating by the shore, he bent down and picked it up. It was the red-and-orange woollen baby hat that Molly had knitted. Despite the cold, tears burned his cheeks.

"Ruth?"

She rushed past him and dived into the water. He called her back. The lizard had gone, and she was putting herself in danger, too. But when she surfaced, his heart jumped.

Ruth walked out of the water holding his son.

## 30

Amelia sat with her back against the battlement as wind gusted around her, but she knew the true storm was still to come. The lizard watched them while the men spoke. Their ceremonial gowns lay on the ground, and they were now dressed in black. She shivered as the cold wind blew a fresh flurry of snow into her face.

"Jack?"

He sat next to her with a bloody face and injured leg.

"Why did you come?"

"I had to do something." He looked at her closely. "Did you send me those feelings?"

She regretted what she'd done. She'd risked the life of a good man. "I'm sorry I involved you."

He shook his head. "I make my own decisions. And at least I took one of them out of the fight."

"Angel?"

He nodded.

"Did you kill him?"

"No, but he's in worse shape than me. The panther

dragged him away. They're probably still on the island somewhere."

"The man has a special connection with the animal."

"They're killers," Jack said.

She nodded. "We've lost Molly and Luke."

"We don't know that," Jack said.

He seemed impossibly positive given the situation, but it made her feel better.

"Who do you think they are?" Jack asked.

She looked at the magicians. The feeling radiating from them was toxic. Of the two, Nimori possessed more power. She could feel it. "I know they're not from this world, and I know their magic is real."

She looked at him, waiting for his reaction. He was hard to read.

"I'm reassessing my thoughts about what they are," he said. "I'd assumed they were foreign agents; I'm less sure now."

"What changed your mind?" she asked.

"The talking lizards. What country has the technology to genetically engineer intelligent lizards?"

A tremor shook the tower.

"My visions show an orange storm engulfing our world," she said. They always end with an image of a burning Earth."

"Invasion?" he asked.

"My guides told me they'd invade, but that the invasion would be the least of our problems." She had his complete attention. "They said the invasion would be forgotten after a couple of centuries, that we'd be entranced by their technology."

"That may be true," Jack said, "but I don't want to live

through it. If invasion's the lesser problem, what's the greater one?"

"The things that would come with them from the space between worlds."

The lizard moved, and she looked up. It hissed at her. She quickly covered her face, feeling the light spray of its spittle burn her skin.

"Don't make eye contact with it," Jack said.

She spat on the backs of her hands and rubbed them on her jeans. "Do you think it's an animal?"

"Only in the sense that we all are," Jack said.

"They act intelligent," she said, taking care not to make eye contact. Despite its ferocity, its energy didn't have the toxicity of the two sorcerers.

"They can speak," Jack said. "It may be able to understand what we're saying now."

The lizard turned and walked to the trapdoor, which opened as it reached it.

"Its listening must be incredible," she whispered.

She watched a man climb onto the roof. He was wearing a police uniform.

"Inspector Gully," Jack said. "He was taken from the grounds of the manor."

A procession of five bedraggled women and a man followed him. The lizard pointed Gully towards them but made the women and man sit further away. They looked ill.

Gully nodded.

"Are you okay?" Jack asked.

"They treated me well." He glanced at the line of shivering women and the man. "Better than them by the looks of it. I had a cold room in the tower, but they fed me well. Wine, too."

Amelia wondered why. "What did they say to you?"

"Nothing really, but they visited me every few hours. It was sort of weird. Sometimes they'd just sit and stare at me for thirty or forty minutes at a time. Especially Olney."

"Any ideas?" Jack asked Amelia.

"Why would she?" Gully asked.

Jack shrugged. Gully walked over to the women and started asking them questions.

"Some sort of mind control, perhaps," she whispered.

"Why do you think they didn't just kill us?" he asked.

"Do you remember the green light Luke reported when Leander Amis was dying?" Amelia asked.

"I read about it. Why?"

"I'm not sure what sort of things you believe, but that was part of his vital energy. They're taking it from people," she whispered, afraid the two men would hear.

"Do you really believe that?" Jack asked quietly.

"I do."

Jack glanced at the women and man. "They look drained of energy."

She nodded.

"Why do all this?"

"To add power to their magic," she said. "To help in whatever they plan to do at sunrise."

Jack studied her expression for several seconds. "I don't claim to understand any of this, but when you did your stuff—"

"You mean when I tried to contact you?"

He nodded. "Did you do the same to Luke?"

"I tried, but he was too dense." She smiled. "You're strong, but quite sensitive, too. You were my best hope."

But with Jack unarmed and injured, she knew they had little chance of escaping by themselves. Both of the magicians were armed, but even unarmed they were deadly. And they had magic. She felt it pressing against her; it wasn't even subtle. The magicians stopped talking and walked towards them. She studied their features. Apart from their height and their intensity, the only thing unusual was the angular shape of their heads. It wasn't so strange—they'd blend in perfectly with commuters on the London Underground—but now she looked closely, she saw the similarity between them. She had the feeling that they'd decided on something.

"Why are we here?" she asked.

"I think you already know part of that," Nimori said. He watched her closely as if he were reading her like a book. "Tell us what we want to know. It won't be so bad for you."

"A quick death?"

The man ignored her comment. "Olney told me you were doing things you shouldn't, that you summoned a witch. It's time to dig deeper."

He spoke to Olney in his language, but a screech from the lake distracted him, and he walked to the battlement with one of the lizards. Olney touched her, and she shuddered. It was slightly preferable to only have one of them there, but she still desperately wanted to avoid this. Thinking of anything she could say as a distraction, she remembered what Jack had said about Angel.

"Where's Angel?" She looked around. "He's one of you, too."

"Dead, for all I care," Olney said.

"And the panther?"

"It's not important. Not now."

*Now the hunting's done*, she thought. "You seem very relaxed for someone surrounded," Amelia said. Olney didn't reply, and she wiped more of the gritty snow from her face.

The back of her hand was covered in sand. Much more than normal. "Where's this stuff coming from?"

He called Nimori over, then taking her hand and turning it around, he grinned at the man. Again, they spoke in their language. Nimori turned, speaking to the lizard as Frank Olney pulled her to her feet.

"Leave her!" Jack said. "Take me instead."

She noticed that Inspector Gully said nothing. He cowered near the line of women and the other man.

Olney gave a short laugh. "You don't have what she does." He dragged her away from Jack and thrust her against the ramparts, squeezing her throat where her skin was already grazed. "Stop struggling and it'll be easier for you."

She pressed herself harder against the ramparts, and she felt his cold mind enter hers, taking over her body. She choked as she lost control of her own breathing, and she felt her face turning blue.

"Let her breathe!" Nimori ordered.

Amelia wondered if Frank Olney was the sorcerer's apprentice. He was younger, although not a young man, perhaps in his mid-thirties. Suddenly her body functions returned to her control, and she gasped for breath.

"Search her memories," Nimori said. "Woman, let him in, or I'll join him, and you won't like that."

She believed him but didn't respond. It seemed that he was teaching Olney, and she was the subject of the class. She didn't want the master entering, too.

"What are you doing to her?" Jack asked, but there was no answer, apart from a dull thump, which she guessed was a kick.

Olney searched her childhood memories, but he searched haphazardly. He moved rapidly through the years, and she saw memories flick before her eyes as if she were looking at a series of photographs taken at special times in her life. He stopped in her friends' house in Clapham Common.

Olney spoke in their language; Nimori looked up.

Amelia tried to push him out, but he mentally slapped her, and she was almost paralysed with fear. She stopped struggling and watched her own memories as if she were an observer. He watched the summoning again. She detected fear, but it made no sense. Why were they afraid of her and not the military? Olney shook his head and continued to speak. He sounded agitated.

"What did the witch say?" Nimori asked her. His voice took on an edge of concern. "What are you hiding?"

She almost felt like laughing. This evil man was scared of her when all she could do was hide in her own mind. But then she realised that it wasn't her that scared him. Amelia thought about the witch. Her burning eyes still unnerved her. She knew the witch wanted these men dead; she sensed her on the edges of her mind but dreaded her presence and wished her away. The feeling of the alien witch lessened, but she was still sweating, and her body shook—she didn't want this. As she felt their energy, she started to suspect that they were much stranger than she'd thought.

"You've made a connection," Olney said. His face showed both disgust and fear.

The presence of the witch on the fringes of her mind was more subtle than that of the man in front of her. Nimori came closer and said something. When Olney didn't respond, Nimori slapped him, but the man was stuck to her like a leech. Nimori pulled out a pistol—he was going to execute her.

"No!" Jack shouted.

Amelia felt close to panic. She was almost locked out of her own mind, and these men wanted to murder her.

"*Give yourself to me,*" the witch's voice murmured in her mind.

"*Why do you even ask?*" Amelia said.

"*Open yourself to me!*"

"*What will happen?*" Amelia asked.

"*You'll become a weapon.*" She felt Olney begin to withdraw.

"*Now!*"

Amelia saw the gun aimed at her head. She had nothing to lose.

"*Do what you want.*"

Amelia felt as if she fell into a swirling vortex; the air was sucked away, and she almost passed out. Then she fully ceded control, and a fiery presence entered her body. She was now an observer connected to her body by a mere thread.

Frank Olney screamed in terror.

She realised she was squeezing his throat. He gasped, and she shuddered at his scream. She felt something being ripped from his body. And then it was gone. Olney's corpse lay at her feet, and Nick Nimori stared at her in terror.

"Do you remember me?"

She spoke in a language she'd never learnt, but she understood every word. Nimori stepped backwards but was hesitant to shoot. Amelia wasn't sure why until the witch spoke through her again.

"If you shoot her body, I'll come for yours."

A fiery wisp stretched from Amelia's hand towards Nimori. The man paled and stepped backwards. Amelia followed him, but the witch wasn't in complete control of her body, and she staggered like some strange zombie. She was aware of Jack staring at her with his mouth wide open.

"This can't be possible," Nimori said in the same strange language.

Somehow, Amelia understood.

"Many things are possible," the witch said. "I can reach you here."

Amelia was breathing heavily, and she felt a pounding headache begin.

"What do you want?"

"You know what I want," the witch said.

Nimori looked around the top of the tower, and noticing the reptile staring at Amelia, he ordered it to kill her, but it backed away with a whispering hiss.

"It's wiser than you," the witch said.

"Why do you even care about all of this?" Nimori asked.

"Because I do."

Nimori backed away.

"Come to me!"

Nimori shook his head and stepped further back.

Amelia watched the world as if through another's eyes. She felt faint. Then, on hearing a cry, she turned and saw Inspector Gully fall to the floor. He seemed to be having some sort of epileptic fit. A thud made her turn back. Jack had rolled along the ground and kicked Nimori in the back of his knee. The sorcerer fell to the ground, and Jack took his pistol.

The lizard remained stationary as if made of stone.

Amelia found herself turning towards the creature, and again she was compelled to speak in a language she didn't understand, but this time she really didn't understand. Jack later told her that the lizard had appeared rapt as it had listened. All she saw was the lizard bowing its head towards her before leaping over the top of the ramparts. One of the commandos surrounding the island later told her that it had run straight down the outside of the tower and dived into the lake. It hadn't attacked them.

Then the witch spoke to her. *"I'm being pulled away by magic stronger than me."*

*"Can you help us?"* Amelia asked.

*"I helped counter a magic that should never have entered your world. That's all. You're strong enough to finish it."*

*"What should I do?"*

*"Kill him."*

The witch's presence gradually faded until only a faint smouldering impression remained in her mind. Nimori sat up and drew a second pistol from the pile of discarded ceremonial robes.

"That thing's gone, and without it, you're nothing."

Before Nimori could pull the trigger, a shot rang out, and he collapsed. Jack had shot him in his side. He took the man's second gun.

"Don't kill him," Amelia said, ignoring the witch's advice. "We may be able to learn something from him."

As Jack searched him again for other weapons, Nimori smirked. She shivered. He seemed too confident for someone who'd just been shot and captured. The tower shook. The tremors were becoming more frequent. Shots sounded from the island, and a minute later commandos stormed onto the roof.

"Too late," Jack said with a grin. "But the hostages need help getting off the island."

One of the commandos nodded at him, and soon the line of women, the man, and Inspector Gully filed down the steps. Nimori was handcuffed. He climbed unsteadily down the steps in front of them. Amelia was surprised he could still walk. Jack kept his pistol on the man's back. Three inflatables waited on the shore. Marines put Nimori into one of them, which immediately headed back towards the manor. Luke sat in the second with his son in his arms.

Ruth waited in the final inflatable, and when she saw Jack, she jumped out to help him. A commando helped Amelia into the boat, and they waited for the final marine who was pulling the body of the boatman behind him—the same boatman who'd taken Angel to the tower. The water swished from side to side in the lake, sending waves rolling towards the shore. The tremors were increasing. After the commando lifted the boatman's body into the boat, they turned for the shore. Ruth leant forward and studied the boatman's body as the boat rose in the swell. She narrowed her eyes, and then she looked at Jack and Amelia.

"What?" Amelia asked.

She pointed at the body, but Amelia couldn't see anything wrong.

Jack shrugged.

Ruth pointed at his nose. "He has gills."

## 31

As Amelia stood in the damp library, hearing things she probably shouldn't, she began to realise the extent of her naivety. She'd innocently thought that the authorities would believe they were dealing with aliens after Ruth had discovered that the men possessed gills. But they didn't. Only she was convinced. Although Jack was coming to believe it. And only she understood the threats they posed for the planet. After the release of the hostages, the deaths of two of the enemy, and the capture of Nick Nimori, the authorities appeared to think the crisis was over.

The four of them—her team as she now saw them—remained silent. She was thankful that Luke's young son, who was strapped close to his chest, was sleeping peacefully. None of them wanted to be ordered out. This was too important. But they stood on the sidelines. Two new MI5 agents, John Smith and Emma Jackson, had arrived to oversee the government orders.

"Can we say the language is a dialect of Russian?" John Smith asked.

Several people looked towards Luke. He sighed. Amelia wondered if these agents had read the reports.

"No," Luke said. "We cannot. It's unlike any language I've heard."

"I thought you were an expert," Smith said.

"I am."

"He's still under arrest for possible collusion with the foreign power," Emma Jackson said.

Smith nodded. "It may not be in his interest to tell us."

"I'm not one of them," Luke said. "And I'm not the only linguist to have listened to the language. Find a Russian speaker who'll tell you it's a dialect of Russian."

"We already have a trained linguist fluent in Russian speaking to the prisoner," Smith said.

"And?" Luke asked.

"The prisoner's not cooperating yet, but we'll persist."

"They're aliens," Amelia said.

"I don't see any antennae sticking out of their heads," Smith said.

"They have gills."

"Which shows incredible skill in genetic engineering," Emma Jackson said. "Wherever they come from, we have some scientific catching up to do. This could be a great opportunity for our country."

"We have things to do, but I think we can agree that the crisis is over," Smith said. "Now we must focus on mopping up and discovering what exactly they've built at the bottom of the lake."

"The crisis is not over!" Amelia exclaimed.

She'd spoken louder than she'd intended, but she was scared by this cavalier attitude. The vision of an alien world and the warnings from her spirit guides were still in her mind.

"The foreign agents are dead or captured," Jackson said. "And the structure beneath the lake appears entirely passive. There's no indication that anyone's inside it."

"My wife may be inside," Luke said. He patted his son, who had just woken up. "And there may be other hostages."

Inspector Gully, who had been sitting quietly in the corner, came to life at the mention of hostages. "We've recovered all of the hostages."

"How do you know?" Luke asked.

"Frank Olney told me that anyone who escaped would be returned to the underwater station and executed." He looked at Luke. "I'm sorry, but your wife is dead."

"You believed him?" Superintendent Dale asked.

"I don't see why he'd lie, and some of the hostages confirmed this when I asked them," Gully said.

Amelia watched Luke's face alter as the news sank in. He held the baby close and closed his eyes. He was shaking. She wanted to speak to him, and wasn't sure that Gully was telling the truth, but she had to focus on the meeting. "It's not just the aliens," Amelia said. Smith curled his lips when she spoke. "It's what will come from between the worlds. Even they're unaware of what might come with them."

"Where's your evidence?"

"My spirit guides told me." She no longer cared what people thought. She had to speak the truth.

He waved her away dismissively with a flick of this wrist. "Spirit guides? Does anyone seriously think we should continue this discussion?"

His colleague, Emma Jackson, smirked.

"The enemy are not all dead or captured," Jack said. "William Angel Provost is loose. And there are the animals."

"We're aware of Provost. The police and military are

doing a sweep of the area. He's injured, and we're confident we'll find him by the morning.

"As far as the animals are concerned, we don't believe this is of primary importance. It seems that the lizards are dead," Smith said. "At least there's no sign of them, although we're requiring the SBS to remain on hand just in case. The panther will be tracked. Teams of dogs are already on the way. It won't escape." The man continued. "Our final task is the salvaging of the structure."

A gust of orange snow blew into the library.

"It's not over," Amelia said. "Even if we've caught them all, they were opening a passage to their home world. We still have to stop that." She looked at her watch. "We have forty minutes till dawn—a little longer until sunrise." She paused, not wanting to upset Luke further, but she knew she had to say what was on her mind. "We must destroy the structure."

"Why is a fortune teller even here?" Smith glanced at the others.

Amelia bristled. She didn't even believe in fortune telling—not in the way most people thought of it. Her own aggressive stance also surprised her. She was usually more peaceful, but the messages from her guides had frightened her.

"She's been accurate so far," Jack said.

"I've read the reports, and the truth of what happened is yet to be determined. As is who she is," Smith said. "I'll remind you that you've been suspended from the Security Service and have no say in any of this. All four of you were only brought here for your skills and the information you possessed. As the hostage situation has been resolved, you're no longer needed."

He looked at Superintendent Dale. "Dr Lee and Ms Blake are still under arrest." Dale nodded.

"Ms Hardy, thank you for your help, but your services are no longer required. You are to return to London immediately." Ruth glanced at her field laboratory. "Leave your samples and equipment here. We'll deal with it."

The meeting was over, and Superintendent Dale called a constable into the room.

"I'm sorry," Superintendent Dale said, looking at Amelia and Luke. "You're still technically under arrest for serious crimes. We need to question you, and it may take quite some time."

Then Superintendent Dale turned to Jack. "Mr Ross, I also have to detain you for questioning over the theft of a firearm and canoe."

Looking to one of the police officers, Dale said, "Put them in one of the vans. We'll take them to the station later."

"You need us!" Amelia said. "The four of us know more than anyone about the enemy."

"She has a point," Captain Willis said. "I've been ordered to remain until we've secured the structure and are sure it's safe. And I've been authorised to requisition any resources I need to do my job. I'm requisitioning this team of four experts."

Superintendent Dale glanced at the MI5 agents. They nodded.

"Very well, Captain. You can take responsibility for them."

Three of the experts walked to the end of the garden; Luke had gone in search of milk and warmer clothing for the baby. None of them felt welcome inside the library. The naval unit had brought searchlights, which now swept over the lake, only partially penetrating the fog. They watched the naval personnel checking an unmanned underwater vehicle that hung beneath one of the Merlins. It looked like a torpedo to Amelia.

"This is a bad idea," she said.

"I agree," Jack said.

The helicopter lifted off, moving slowly over the lake towards the larger of the two islands, with the torpedo-like vehicle hanging underneath it.

"Where's Nimori?" Amelia asked.

"Locked in the wine cellar," Jack said.

"I guess he's having a good time," Ruth said.

"It's empty."

"I heard Amis was a wine connoisseur."

"That's probably why one of his relatives came here this morning and emptied it."

"If he's not drinking wine, what's he doing?" Amelia asked.

"Acting strange," Jack said. "No one's been able to get near him."

She frowned. "What do you mean?" She was scared he'd use magic whether anyone believed in it or not.

"His guards complained of feeling nauseous. When they moved away from the cellar, they recovered."

"Anything else?" Amelia asked.

"They complained their vision became cloudy. That they couldn't think properly." Jack looked at Amelia. "Any ideas?"

"He can enter a person's mind and manipulate it. Perhaps we should have killed him on the tower like the witch wanted."

"You know we couldn't do that," Jack said.

"We might pay for it later." Amelia was half regretting

her softness, but Jack was right. They couldn't just go around killing people.

She shivered as a cold breeze blew across the lake. The underwater vehicle dropped into the water. There were still thirty minutes until dawn. Now they had to wait.

Jack guessed her thoughts. "Waiting is part of the game, but if anything we've learnt is correct, something will happen soon. Maybe too much."

Ruth bent down and picked up something from the snow. She held it up. Amelia wrinkled her nose at what looked like a giant woodlouse. It was about nine inches long.

"At least it's dead," Amelia said, studying the creature.

"A door to another world would explain creatures like this," Ruth said.

"Do you believe it now?" Jack asked.

"I don't know, but I'm considering all options." She put the woodlouse in a plastic bag, adding it to her samples.

Raised voices came from the library.

"Let's see what's happening?" Jack suggested.

They returned to the library. Luke was already there with a well-wrapped baby and a bottle of milk. Captain Willis was ordering his men out; they were setting up a base in the military vehicles by the lake. More government agents had arrived and were setting up on the long table.

But one young naval lieutenant was still working on a laptop. He interrupted them. "We're getting visuals on the underwater structure."

They gathered round to look.

The structure was nothing like Amelia had expected. For some reason, she'd imagined an underwater dome, but this was a sleek metal structure.

"What do you make of it?" Jackson asked.

"I've never seen anything like it," Captain Willis said. "It would help if we could see the whole structure."

"Go closer," Smith said.

The lieutenant controlling the device nodded, sending it right up to the alien structure.

"Incredible," Smith said.

The image disappeared.

"What happened?"

The lieutenant frantically tried to re-establish contact with the device, but the screen remained blank. "The controls seem to be functioning, but something's happened to the camera."

"You went in too close," Jackson said.

The lieutenant glared at her for a second and then returned to the laptop.

"Bring it back," Captain Willis said. "We'll check the camera."

Smith answered his phone, wandering off to a private corner of the library.

"What are they doing?" Jack asked.

The captain shrugged. "They call Thames House every few minutes, and they're in constant touch with the government. Expect more stupidity from Whitehall."

The lieutenant looked up and grinned before returning to his laptop. "It's surfacing now."

Captain Willis went outside, and the others followed, to look at the underwater vehicle. The naval crew helped attach cables to it, and ten minutes later it was sitting on the narrow beach. A seaman pointed at the digital camera.

"It's been smashed."

"How?" Luke asked.

The sailor shrugged. "It hit something..."

An order came from the command centre in the library.

Divers were to be sent down to the structure accompanied by the underwater vehicle, once a new camera had been attached. A team of six divers, all wearing dry suits, was getting ready. When a new camera was attached, the divers left in two inflatables, and the four experts went back to the library. Amelia was glad she wasn't diving through the cold murky water. Again, she watched the structure appear on the laptop. Visibility was poor at the bottom of the mere, but the metal structure still looked impressive.

"The structure still appears to be dead. Nothing is happening inside," the lieutenant said. "No sounds at all."

The images were being simultaneously sent to London, and Smith received another short call. Amelia heard him mention cranes. It looked like they were going to attempt to lift it from the lake bed.

"What the . . ." the naval lieutenant started.

A lizard swam towards the divers. They backed away, and the lieutenant tried to manoeuvre the underwater vehicle towards the creature, attempting to use it as a weapon.

"Get to the surface!" Willis ordered all divers.

The next image shocked the viewers. A dozen swimming lizards followed the divers.

"They need help," Jack said. "Send in a helicopter to pick up anyone who makes it to the surface."

Captain Willis nodded and made the order.

Several seconds later, the rotor blades of one of the Merlins started to turn. Amelia watched the screen go blank again. They'd lost contact with two divers. The image returned when the lieutenant switched back to the underwater vehicle's camera. It was hard to make much out, except that the lizards pursued the divers. She could hardly stand watching. She looked away and prayed for them.

When she looked again, she saw a lizard swimming directly at the underwater vehicle, and then the screen went blank.

"We've lost it," the lieutenant said.

"Can you bring it back?" Smith asked.

"No." The man shook his head. "I've lost all communication. It's as if it's not there."

A minute later the Merlin found a diver on the surface, and they dropped a ladder. As the helicopter lifted up, a lizard flew several feet from the surface, snapping at the man. It dropped back into the water with part of his leg in its mouth.

"Sir," the lieutenant said. "Our boats are under attack."

"Bring them back," Captain Willis ordered.

"Captain Willis, what can you do to stop these animals?" Jackson asked.

He looked coldly at her. "We can drop depth charges set to explode above the structure. That should kill them."

Smith spoke again to London. Turning to Willis with the phone still pressed against his ear, he asked, "Won't that damage the structure?"

"Yes, but it'll kill the lizards."

"How much damage will it do?"

"It'll probably put a hole in it, but it won't destroy it."

Smith ended his conversation with London. "Very well. Use depth charges, but use the minimum force necessary. This is too great an opportunity to lose because of a pack of animals."

"What about the men who've lost their lives?" Jack asked.

"That's unfortunate," Smith said as he stared at the monitor.

Amelia was disgusted by the man's attitude.

When the inflatables returned to the shore, Captain

Willis ordered the second Merlin to attack the structure. It flew to the centre of the mere, dropped the charges, and circled back. The explosion sent water pluming into the air.

"Got them," Smith said.

Seconds later, an intense flash of light came from the mere, and the Merlin exploded.

## 32

Dawn had arrived, and with it, a dark swirling spot in the sky. No one in command knew what it was, nor did they know what to do about the structure under the lake.

The dark spot was growing.

Luke watched the patch of intense darkness through a pair of binoculars he'd found in the library. He was worried and now believed Amelia, as did Jack and Ruth. But not many others were convinced, despite the growing evidence supporting her. The flickering dots of light within the darkness were not so easy to explain away, nor the high-tech weapons used against the helicopter, nor the creatures, the gills, or the language.

This was real, and Luke thought of ways to stop the enemy while people rushed around him frantically. In the minds of the military, it was war, and Luke would support them in any way he could. His three friends would do the same. It was clear that the structure beneath the lake was not passive. The military had been attacked, and they wanted revenge. He wanted the same. For Molly, and for his son, who would never know his mother.

Amazingly, his son still slept against his chest. And although Luke couldn't fight as these commandos could, he could fight with his mind. If the enemy wanted to escape, as Amelia said, he was determined to stop them. The serious reasons she gave were almost superfluous. He was amazed that the government agents, Smith and Jackson, had suggested that if the enemy were really aliens, then they should let them go because of the damage they might cause.

Ruth was sitting on a chair someone had requisitioned from the manor with her laptop on her lap, intensely working on something. Curious, Luke walked over to her. Perhaps there was some way he could help.

"What are you working on?"

"We have monitoring stations set up in the local area to monitor the amount of sand falling from the sky. I'm measuring its rate of increase."

"What have you found?"

"The rate of increase is slowing," Ruth said. "If this pattern continues, then it might indicate that the hole in the sky will be at its widest in about forty-five minutes from now."

"At sunrise?" he asked.

She nodded. "If I'm right, then it'll begin to reduce in size after that point."

"So that's the time we have to stop them escaping," Luke said.

She nodded hesitantly. "Possibly. It seems logical that if they're going to escape it'd be when the hole is at its largest. But there's no way I can know for sure."

Captain Willis, Jack, and Amelia were listening to the

conversation, as were two technicians working in the back of the vehicle.

A bleep came from one of the technician's laptops. "I have a radio signal," he said.

"From the structure under the lake?" Amelia asked.

"I presume so."

"Can we listen," Luke said.

The man played a recording of the strange language.

"It's them!" Luke said. "Play it again." He focussed all his attention on the recording.

"I get the gist of it," Luke said, glancing at Ruth. "They're calling home."

"Their world?" Ruth asked.

He nodded. "They say they're coming through at sunrise. Exactly when you expect the hole to be at its widest."

"They're making no movement at the moment," Willis said.

"We don't know how they'll attempt to escape," Jack said. "They're stuck at the bottom of the lake in a static structure, but the hole's in the sky."

"They might have rockets," Luke said.

"If they send up rockets, we'll shoot them down," Willis said. He started giving instructions to his men.

"Look at the lake," Amelia said.

It was frothing and bubbling. Steam rose into the cold dawn sky. While the others went to look, Luke sat on another chair in the garden and thought of ways to stop the enemy from leaving. Perhaps shooting down the rockets, if that's what they used, would work.

Luke became more determined to stop them. Whatever they wanted, he wanted to prevent. "I have a question."

The radio technician looked up.

"If I wanted to send a radio message to the enemy asking them to delay their departure, could I make it appear as if it came from the dark spot in the sky?"

"We could attach a radio to one of the drones that have just come in, then we could fly it near the darkness and then send it from there. But they'd see the drone."

"Would they be able to detect the location if we sent a radio transmission from here?" Luke asked.

"Yes, if they have the right equipment, and if they bothered to search for the location. But if they were expecting a message to come from the dark spot, then perhaps we could trick them."

That was all Luke needed.

He picked up one of the laptops he'd been using and started to compose a message to the aliens in their own language.

AMELIA WANDERED BACK to the lake with Jack. She hoped Luke's idea would work, but they needed to do more to ensure success.

"Do you really think we could cause an explosion by trying to stop them?" she asked. "Similar to Battersea?"

Jack grinned. "Perhaps. That's part of the job, but I'd take the risk to stop an invasion."

A marine ran to the command post.

"Captain Willis."

The captain looked up. "Yes?"

"There's a problem with the prisoner."

Amelia had a sinking feeling—something was wrong. She thought back to what Jack had said about Nimori's guards having hallucinations.

"What problem?"

"The interpreter and the guards walked out of the manor. They seemed to be sleepwalking. When we woke them up, they collapsed. They're unconscious now. Inspector Gully is looking over the situation, but he's acting strange, too."

Amelia knew that Captain Willis needed all the men he had by the lake.

"We can go," she said, glancing questioningly at Jack.

Jack nodded. He was armed and as capable as any of the marines, although his injuries slowed him a little.

"Very well. Report back when you discover what's happening."

They ran to the annex, where the wine cellar was housed. Two guards and the interpreter lay on the snow outside. A medic attended them.

"How are they?" she asked.

"Recovering slowly."

"Where's Gully?"

"Inside and acting odd," the medic said.

Jack rushed inside the manor kitchen. Amelia ran after him.

Inspector Gully walked out of the open doorway at the top of the stairs leading to the cellar. He appeared in a daze.

"Inspector Gully?" Amelia said, but he didn't respond.

"That door should be locked," Jack said.

"Someone's coming up the stairs!" She quickly stepped back.

Nick Nimori walked out of the doorway to the cellar. Jack pointed his assault rifle at the man, but Nimori raised his hand, and Jack collapsed, his gun clattering onto the stone floor. Amelia backed away. The hair on her body stood on end as magic crackled around him. An unseen punch knocked her to the ground, and as light flickered in her eyes, she tried to focus on the pale blue ceiling. She didn't want to faint. She could hardly breathe as an immense pressure pushed down on her chest, almost suffocating her. This was the last thing she wanted. This monster forcing his way into her mind. She thought she was passing out, but then, the still smouldering impression the witch had left in her mind glowed orange. The familiar presence returned.

*"I never completely left you,"* the Orange Witch whispered. *"I knew you wouldn't kill him."*

*"Help me!"* Amelia gasped. She was only aware of the terrible pressure of the sorcerer, the cold kitchen floor, and the whispering witch. She could feel the witch do something but couldn't tell exactly what.

The pressure on her chest eased, and she breathed more easily.

*"What's this?"* Nimori asked, sensing something.

*"I've come to kill you,"* the witch said.

*"You!"*

The Orange Witch reached towards the sorcerer's mind, but he resisted. Amelia's body jerked on the floor as the two practitioners of magic fought. It was the worst experience she'd ever had. Her heart felt as if it were being ripped from her chest—she was having a heart attack.

*"Join your force with mine,"* the witch whispered in her mind.

Amelia wasn't sure how, but as the witch seemed the lesser of two evils, she lent what energy she had to the witch. The shocking pain in her heart disappeared.

She sat up and stared at the dishevelled magician, who was slumped over the heavy wooden kitchen table. He was motionless.

*"Stand!"* the witch said.

"*Don't make me kill him,*" Amelia said, terrified the witch would force her to take a kitchen knife and slaughter the man.

The witch laughed. "*You need to become stronger.*"

Amelia walked to the table. She prodded the man, and he stirred. Again she felt the witch control her movements, but there was no attempt to use her to kill the man. Instead, the witch spoke through her in the strange language.

Nimori turned to look at her; blood ran from his mouth.

Thinking she was fainting, Amelia grasped the table hard. She lost sight of the kitchen, and everything went black. Then she saw a dark energetic image before her. It was Nimori. She realised that he was attacking her again.

Magic threads pulsed from his fingers and reached for her, but fire from the witch rushed through her, burning the threads and leaving a putrid smell in the room. The witch burst the magic bubble around him and propelled her into Nimori's mind. The magician gasped.

"*See and believe,*" the witch whispered.

Amelia accompanied the witch into the magician's mind. She saw the dark hole in the sky, and together they rushed into the hole and through a long tunnel. Sparks flew from the sides of the tunnel, and minutes seemed to pass. Then they reached the other end.

She stood in a desert. A bright sun shone down. A shining city rose before her, and men watched her; they reminded her of the magicians. They seemed to speak to her, but she soon realised that they'd been speaking to Nimori. This was a memory of his planet—a hot, arid desert world.

"*This is another version of Earth,*" the witch whispered. "*He's made contact, and the door is open.*"

Amelia saw sand being sucked into the hole at the other

end, and she understood where the orange sand and exotic creatures came from.

*"How did they open it?"* she asked.

The question led her to another memory. Women were bleeding, and their ectoplasmic energy helped form the connection with the other world. Then she saw a larger version of the machine she'd seen in the house in Battersea. They'd used a combination of black magic and technology.

Then she saw an army waiting in the desert.

Nimori fought back, and Amelia felt herself pushed from his mind.

Gasping, she opened her eyes.

Nimori laughed. "The witch has really gone this time."

It was true. Amelia couldn't sense her anywhere. She was alone.

"I've not gone anywhere," Jack said. He looked like he'd been in a violent fight. He had a black eye, and blood ran from his nose. He reached for the pistol in his holster but fumbled taking it out.

Nimori sprinted out of the kitchen door. Jack tried to follow, but he fell against the table. Amelia helped him up, but by the time they'd stepped outside, Nimori had reached the lake. He ran straight into the water and disappeared.

"Jack. We really have a big problem," Amelia said. "I've seen the invasion force."

"It's not me you have to convince," he said.

They helped each other to the command post behind the manor. She noticed the arrival of reinforcements.

"What happened to you?" Captain Willis asked.

Ruth rushed over to Jack, checking his cuts and bruises. Then she looked closely at Amelia.

"I don't know which of you looks worse," she said.

Both Amelia and Jack explained their parts of the story.

"They won't get away," the captain said. "The Army's arrived, and the Air Force will be here soon. We're about to attack."

That made Amelia feel a little better. She looked for Luke. He still had his head down, working hard on the laptop. She turned back to the lake. The dawn was lightening the sky, and soon the sun would rise.

The Merlin lifted off the ground and moved towards the lake. The helicopter was armed with four Stingray torpedoes. Along the shoreline, commandos moved heavy machine guns into position.

"Attack!" Captain Willis ordered. "Use all torpedoes."

The helicopter accelerated fast over the mere, fired all torpedoes, then turned back for the shore. Water cascaded into the air as the Stingrays exploded beneath the mere.

A muted cheer went up from the marines.

The cheers faded to confusion as the water changed colour, glowing in shades of red, orange, and yellow. Amelia willed the helicopter to get away from the lake before anything could happen. A flash of light came from the lake, catching the tail of the helicopter. She watched it spin round and then crash into the water near the shore.

Amelia felt the shock of the men around her. The shock was deepened when she looked up into the sky. The dark spot was now a gaping hole.

"The sun's rising," Jack said.

She shivered. Something was about to happen.

"Sir," a computer operator said. "The underwater structure appears intact and is moving to the surface."

A Wildcat returned from its reconnaissance around the lake. "Load it with anti-surface missiles, and get it ready to fly immediately!" Willis said. "Machine guns on the shore, get ready to fire!"

"It's coming," a marine shouted.

The water frothed, and steam rose from the lake. Red and blue lights lit the water.

"What is it?" Amelia asked. Although she knew the answer as soon as she'd spoken.

They stared at a long white vessel with dark burns along its side. It had fins underneath, and lights flashed along the side. At the front was a long spearlike projection.

"A spaceship," Captain Willis said.

## 33

Luke finished creating his message in the alien language. It was imperfect, but the best he could do. He joined the rest of his team on the shore. Along with over a hundred regular infantry and commandos, they stared at the spaceship rising from the lake. It glistened as water ran from its sleek white body.

Its loudspeakers crackled alive. Luke recognised the voice. He glanced at his friends.

"It looks like Nimori made it back."

They nodded, but their faces showed concern.

"As is obvious," Nimori said in accented English. "We're not from round here." The crackling didn't disguise the laughter in the background. "The good news for you is that we're leaving, and we're pleased to leave peacefully. No one else need die."

"We must stop them," Amelia said, but Luke noticed that no one apart from Captain Willis, Jack, Ruth and himself was listening to her.

Government agents Smith and Jackson were there, as were all the other senior members of the military and police. Jackson was immediately on the phone to London. Luke wondered how they'd react to the alien message. He hoped they wouldn't agree to just let them go.

Smith spoke using loudspeakers set up on the remains of the lawn. "You must surrender. We will ensure you're treated with proper dignity. As a first encounter between species, this got off to a rocky start, but we're prepared to talk."

"We don't wish to chat. For your own safety, I advise you to withdraw your military forces. No one wants an accident to occur."

Jackson, who was still speaking on the phone, glanced at Smith and shook her head.

"We need you to surrender. I'm sorry, but you cannot leave. At least, not yet."

A pair of fighters flew towards the lake, and Luke was pleased, and a little proud, that the military had responded so fast. With the reinforcements, which included an infantry platoon, as well as two more Wildcats, he felt more confident that they could stop the spaceship leaving and prevent the disaster Amelia had predicted.

His pride turned to shock when two flashes of light shot from the spaceship. The fighters exploded in mid-air. The military retaliated immediately. Dozens of rockets exploded against the side of the ship. Smoke rose from some parts of the ship. Again, the spaceship reacted. A dozen or more flashes of light hit positions around the mere.

He was stunned. All around the lake, men lay dying. Many were calling out for help. In a short attack, they'd killed thirty or forty men and injured many more.

"Where's Ruth?" Jack asked, looking frantically for her.

Luke couldn't see her anywhere. He prayed that she hadn't wandered along the shores of the lake because there was only death there. Their rough base behind the manor was the only place near to the lake not hit directly, although several men were bleeding from being hit by flying shrapnel.

"She said she was going to get something from the manor," Amelia said.

Jack began to move towards the manor when a flash of light hit it. The roof exploded and then burst into flames. Jack gasped and his face paled. Luke reached out to steady him.

"If they've hurt her, I'll kill every one of them," Jack said.

Luke felt the same.

Thick clouds of grey smoke came from the burning manor. Someone was running towards them, carrying a box. Luke strained to see through the smoke.

"It's Ruth," Luke said.

She rushed from the manor, her face blackened with dirt from the smoke. Jack sprinted to her.

"Ruth! What did you think you were doing?"

She tried to speak but coughed instead. When Jack tried to help with the box, she moved it away, keeping a tight grip. Ruth glanced back at the burning manor. "I didn't know it was going to be hit," she gasped.

Smith conferred with one of his team members. "Two people are missing. They were deeper inside the house."

Wind blew from the lake, sending the smoke away from them. Luke breathed more comfortably. Emma Jackson, as usual, was on the phone.

"We've been instructed to let them go."

"What?" Captain Willis said. "They've killed over forty of our men!"

"That's why we're letting them go! We want to save lives."

Jackson held out the phone. After a short, frenzied conversation, he handed it back. His eyes were cold.

"We've been ordered to stand down. There's no evidence that an invasion is planned, and nothing to indicate that anything will come through the hole. I've been ordered to only shoot in self-defence."

"Captain . . ." Amelia began, but Willis waved her away.

"There's nothing I can do; it's been decided. If there's really an invasion, then we'll just have to deal with it. To be honest, I don't think anyone in London really believes half the stuff we're saying."

Someone shouted on the far side of the lake, and looking up, Luke saw a bush fly through the air into the hole.

"It's alternating between blowing and sucking," Ruth said.

More small objects had fallen amongst them. Luke looked down at one such fragment of crustacean shell. As Captain Willis turned away, Luke followed him.

"Not now, Luke."

But he persisted, holding out a USB. "I've made an audio recording in their language pretending to be from the other side of the hole. I've instructed them to wait."

"Luke, it's too late—"

"It's not gone yet," Luke said. "Your rockets might have damaged it. Can I give this to your radio operator so he's ready, just in case the situation changes?"

The captain accepted the USB, passing it to one of his men. Then he returned to the injured men by the lake. Amelia was already helping there.

The hole appeared to be breathing with occasional bouts of coughing. Luke comforted his son, who was crying. He didn't like the smoke, and Luke didn't blame him. The injured were being taken to the front of the burning manor; the most seriously injured were being lifted out in one of the Wildcats. He wasn't sure what to do.

The spaceship seemed to be waiting; it was just floating on the lake, but the water around it was frothing and steam rose around it, making it hard to see. Emma Jackson stood beside him looking unhappy.

"Amelia's been right on everything so far. Why won't you accept that?" Luke asked her.

"She's a psychic," Jackson said.

"Perhaps you should open your mind."

A metallic clang came from the top of the spaceship.

Jack and Amelia had rejoined them, and a newly arrived group of medics was dealing with the injured. The dead would have to wait.

"Something's detaching from it," Jack said.

It rose into the air, whining as it approached the dark hole.

"Shoot it down!" Amelia said.

Captain Willis raised his eyebrows. "Do you know what it is?"

"It's almost identical to the device I activated in the house at Battersea," Amelia said. "Except that this one is about ten times bigger."

"But what is it?" the captain asked.

"It's connected to the opening of the portal to their world," Amelia said. She glanced at Luke. "The witch showed me."

It made sense and was what Luke suspected. The alien device hung in the sky beneath the hole.

"It seems to be letting more sand in," Jack said, spitting a mouthful onto the ground. "It's starting to look like we're on the beach."

"Or a desert," Luke said.

Captain Willis had already ordered his men stationed on the far side of the lake to move back. A sandstorm was moving towards them.

"Lizards!" one of the men shouted.

Five lizards with heavy machine guns were about fifty yards to their left. A group of seven commandos faced them. One of the creatures screeched.

"What's happening?" Ruth asked.

Captain Willis shook his head. "Sergeant?"

The sergeant spoke with the men over the radio. "Sir, they say there's something moving in the sky. It's getting closer."

"What about the lizards?"

"They're not threatening the men; they seem to be staring at the thing in the sky."

"I can see it," Ruth said, pointing at the moving object.

A flash of light rushed towards the men and lizards with a plume of bright light stretching out behind it. It hit the ground with a thud. Luke watched through his binoculars as the cloud of dust slowly settled, not understanding what he was seeing.

A tall black creature watched them with blank red eyes. Its ribcage was exposed and on fire.

Luke's skin crawled. He passed the binoculars to Ruth.

"Amelia was right," Ruth said.

The demon shrieked.

## 34

The demon lunged at the nearest lizard, ripping away part of its neck frill. The lizard frantically tried to shake it off, but the demon was stronger, and pulling it closer, it started to feed. Luke shuddered at the lizard's dying screeches. The demon dropped the dead lizard to the ground, and as it did so the fire within it blazed.

"This thing shouldn't exist," Ruth said.

It roared and was answered by something deep within the dark hole in the sky.

"Send the message now!" the captain ordered his radio operator.

He looked the most worried Luke had seen him. "What can we do?" Luke felt helpless. The creature sliced a man in half.

"Follow me," the captain ordered a group of marines. "We're going to kill it."

The captain led a unit of ten men towards it. One carried a flamethrower.

"I'm going to help," Jack said.

"Jack, no!" Ruth said. "It's not your job."

"Protecting my country is my job." He ran towards the battle taking place by the edge of the lake.

"Then I'm going, too," Ruth said. She took two pistols from the outdoor command centre and offered one to Luke.

He took it.

"Luke?" Amelia said. "What about your son?" The baby was awake.

"What kind of life will my son have if things like that invade our world? I'll stand back, but I'll fight if it breaks through."

The three of them followed Jack, who had almost reached the fight. Several dead men and two dead lizards lay beside the lake. When Luke saw the carnage, he started to have second thoughts, but pushing through his fear, he continued to move closer.

"We should have stayed by the manor," Amelia said.

"Perhaps we can help," he said.

"It's starving," Ruth said.

Luke raised his eyebrows. "Well it's taken a few bites of men and lizards."

"No." She pointed towards it. "It's scarred and emaciated. I think it's had a hard life."

Luke almost laughed. Ruth said some strange things sometimes, but she was right. Apart from the open burning ribcage, which he couldn't comprehend at all, its body was extremely thin.

Ruth continued to stare at the demon as it absorbed the bullets; many seemed to pass right through it. Her eyes widened when a marine blasted it with a flamethrower.

"Got it!" the marine shouted.

"Don't be so sure," a lizard hissed.

Luke knew the lizards could speak, but not that they spoke English. And not so clearly.

The demon stared at the flamethrower and the flames within its body raged. It seemed to laugh, and opening a set of dark wings, it flew towards him, smashing his head with a hammer strike.

Luke stepped back from the intense heat.

The demon then ripped apart a dead lizard with its teeth, giving the remaining men and lizards a short rest.

"Is this thing yours?" Jack shouted at the lizards.

The tattooed lizard looked at him. "This thing is not of our world."

Luke watched it carefully. Its blank red eyes glowed, but they were very different from those of a human or the sharp eyes of the lizards. "I'm not sure that it can see very well."

A loud sound from the spaceship distracted them. It was hard to see because of the steam rising around it.

"It's taking off," Jack said.

Captain Willis spoke over the radio and then turned to Luke. "Your message has been sent. I hope it does some good. Now we have to kill this thing."

"I may have an idea," Ruth said.

"Quickly, then!" Captain Willis said.

"I think Luke's right; its eyesight appears to be poor. Its eyes are not adapted to our world. It can hear and smell us, but I don't think it can see us. At least not very well. And it might not have eaten in a very long time. It think it's really hungry."

"So?" the captain said.

She glanced at the lizards, which were staring at her. "It's desperate to eat. If we use drones to lift dead men and lizards towards the hole, it might follow. We'll have to cut the bodies so it can smell the blood." She looked at their blank expressions. "Well, it's just an idea."

"I'm sorry," the captain said, looking at the lizards, "but—"

"Do it!" the tallest of the three lizards hissed.

The spaceship was now rising towards the hole, but several seconds later, it stopped in mid-air. The radio came alive, and Captain Willis answered.

"It seems your message has worked," he said to Luke. "Do you want to hear the ship's reply?"

"Yes," Luke almost shouted.

A message in the alien language played over the radio. Luke frowned as he tried to put the words together.

"I think they're asking why—in not very polite language."

One of the lizards cackled. "You're right, human."

While the demon was finishing the remains of the dead lizard, three military drones flew towards them. The commandos and lizards attached the body of a dead man to one and a dead lizard to another.

Luke looked away. The blood made a gruesome sight.

"Now!" the captain said.

"Hover over the demon," Ruth said.

The captain looked at her.

"We want the blood to drip on it."

The drone with the human remains lifted into the air, but the other struggled to lift the dead lizard's body. The tall lizard slashed the head and tail from its comrade's body, lightening the load. The pair of drones then drifted towards the demon.

Blood rained onto it, and it screeched, its mouth opening wide. When the drones rose to the sky, the demon followed, the fire within its ribcage burning brighter.

"Through the hole," Captain Willis ordered. He turned the radio off and watched.

The demon's wings beat rapidly as the drones flew into the sky. It was gaining on them. The men and lizards watched the pursuit in silence. For a few seconds, Luke was worried that it might catch the drones and return. Then his concern changed. The drones were going to hit the enemy device still hovering beneath the hole.

"That's not good," Amelia said quietly.

But then, seeming to take a dislike to the device, the demon flew faster, reaching the device seconds before the drones. It thrashed out, hitting the humming machine hard, sending it towards the hole.

The demon resumed its pursuit.

Seconds later, the military drones, the demon, and the enemy device were caught up in the storm developing in the sky. They were all were sucked into the dark hole. Lightning flashed from the swirling darkness.

Luke, Amelia, and Ruth moved closer to the others and listened as Captain Willis ordered the third drone into the sky. It was to take images of the hole, hopefully without getting sucked in.

The spaceship's engines screamed as it rose again.

"They're going to try to escape," Luke said. He cried out in shock when something hit his face. Wiping the blood from his cheek, he crouched down to look at a dark object lying in the snow. It was a dead bird, but it was unlike any he'd ever seen.

Ruth pointed at the sky. A flock of birds fell into the mere.

The mixed band of humans and lizards watched the spaceship rise. The winter sun reflected from its bright surface. Under any other circumstances, Luke would have admired its beauty. He held his son tight, but the baby twisted to stare up at the sky. The outer edge of the hole grew darker, but its centre appeared to burn. And then the sky around it tore open, making a ripping sound. The hole grew larger.

"It's opening and closing," Amelia said.

The hole winked like an eye with a bright orange iris. Spouts of water leapt from the centre of the lake, spiralling up into it. Objects rained down, too, especially around the edges of the mere, many of them splashing into the water. A flash of light from the ship destroyed the drone as it approached the hole.

"Open fire!" Captain Willis ordered.

Luke wondered whether the captain had ordered the drone into the sky because he knew the enemy would shoot it down and so give him the excuse to fire in self-defence. If so, he approved.

The heavy machine guns rattled, and small rockets exploded on the side of the ship. It rose unsteadily, stopping, starting, and shaking as it moved. It was heading straight for the hole in the sky. More rockets hit it, and then the ship retaliated. Flashes of light hit gunners' positions around the lake. One hit the remains of the manor, and the building collapsed.

"We've hurt it," Jack said.

The spaceship screeched as it tried to gain altitude. It was desperate to escape. The Wildcats were like metal gnats irritating a huge creature. Distracted, the ship fired at one of the fast-moving helicopters, while another series of small explosions ripped along the surface of the vessel. Then a flash of light hit the helicopter's tail, and it span down into the mere.

The spaceship wobbled more.

Crying out, Luke jumped back as a giant lobster landed feet from him and began crawling towards the frothing water before catching fire. A minute later, nothing remained of the creature. The storm got worse, and the wind whipping around the lake was lifting more objects into the air. On the far side of the lake, a tree flew into the air. Seconds later, Luke saw a dog fly up after it.

The vessel shuddered, and fire spewed from the hole, engulfing the spaceship. The early morning blue turned to burnt orange.

And then the sky exploded.

Luke was thrown to the ground, but he broke his fall with his hands, protecting his crying son. He gasped as the air was sucked from around him. Amelia screamed as she rose into the air. Jack tried to pull Ruth down. She still had the box in her arms. Luke, too, was pulled upwards, rising several inches from the ground.

Then, with a loud crack, the hole snapped shut.

They dropped to the ground as a sandstorm enveloped them. Pain shot through Luke's leg, almost causing him to faint. A jagged piece of metal was sticking out of his thigh. He pulled it out and then wished he hadn't, worried he'd bleed to death, but the blood flow slowed. They slowly stood as the sand swirled around them.

Captain Willis looked at the three remaining lizards.

Luke was ready to fight, but no one moved against the heavily armed creatures.

"I can't see the spaceship," Amelia said, straining to see through the sandstorm. "Or the portal."

"Sand is still coming through," Captain Willis said.

"There's a draught," one of the lizards said.

"What?" the captain snapped.

"Let it speak," Jack said quietly. The captain nodded.

"What do you mean?" Amelia asked.

"Even when closed, there's a draught," it hissed.

"How do you know?" Luke asked.

"Nimori said it," the lizard said.

"He's probably dead by now," the captain said.

The three lizards raised their weapons, cackling when the marines started. "Today we fought together, but tomorrow's another day."

The lizards walked into the sandstorm.

"You're just going to let them go?" the sergeant asked.

Captain Willis shrugged. "Do you want to arrest them?"

The sergeant grinned. "Not today."

Around the lake, marines were coming back to life. There were far fewer than before. Many lay moaning from injuries. The captain and the able-bodied marines started to move the injured back towards the burning manor.

"You're hurt," the captain said to Luke. "Do you need help?"

Luke shook his head. His leg hurt, but he could manage to limp to the front of the manor. He wiped blood from his son's face, relieved to discover that it wasn't the child's. All four of them were bloody, but they could move, if slowly.

"I need to rest," Amelia said several minutes later.

They hadn't moved very far; it was becoming difficult. They sat on a layer of sand and soot that covered a garden wall. Then it started to rain. One man cheered, but within a minute the rain had turned into a torrential downpour, and dirty rivers of mud swept towards the half-empty mere. Amelia grabbed hold of Luke, and he gripped the wall tightly to stop himself being washed into the refilling mere. The fires at least were lessening.

Luke looked up. "The hole's gone." He squinted through the sandstorm. "I think."

"You're right," Jack said.

"And the ship," Ruth said.

Luke couldn't control the tears that ran down his face. His final hope for Molly had gone with the ship.

He felt Amelia squeeze his arm.

They sat there for what felt like hours. Eventually, a medic came and checked them, telling them they were lucky. There were less than thirty men left alive. The medic informed them that a rescue was delayed because of the extreme weather conditions. He covered the baby with a piece of cloth to protect against the sand. The rain had changed, becoming hard and abrasive. It felt like hail. Luke held out his hand, and soon it was full of orange sand. It was becoming hard to breathe, and he covered his mouth. The grass and plants in the garden had disappeared under layers of sand.

"We have to get out of here," Jack said.

They stood and staggered arm in arm towards the front of the remains of the manor. The sand here was much deeper than on the lake side, and its level was rising every few minutes. A constable sat on a chair in front of several vehicles, some of which were overturned.

"It's not safe," a constable said, pointing to the sand dune forming where there had once been a lane. "We're waiting for a road clearing crew."

"It's not safe here either," Amelia said.

It felt surreal to Luke, and he doubted that any road-clearing crew could clear these dunes. No one knew what was about to happen, not with the sandstorm still raging. And none of them was in a mood to wait. The constable said nothing when Amelia walked up to a police car and opened the driver's door.

"I'm driving," Amelia said. "I raced in the Abu Dhabi Desert Challenge five years ago."

"You're our driver," Jack said as he limped to the car.

A whirring sound came from the centre of the mere.

"What's that?" Luke croaked, hardly able to speak from coughing up sand.

An orange tornado rushed around the tower and then veered away over the previously green fields, depositing huge quantities of sand over the land.

"The sand seems to be deeper further away from the lake," Luke said.

"All the more reason to get out of here fast," Jack said.

Luke sat in the passenger seat rocking his son; Ruth and Jack were behind. Amelia seemed to brighten behind the wheel, and her improved mood affected all of them. Luke felt better as she raced up the nearest sand dune and then onward through the changing landscape. What had once been green pastoral countryside had now become a sand dune desert—only the upper parts of a tree and a church spire were visible.

Ruth pulled open her box.

Luke turned stiffly to look.

An extendible eye stalk pushed out of the box. The lobster watched him.

"I sneaked him out," Ruth said.

Luke grinned and realised he'd not felt relaxed enough to smile in days. But then his thoughts returned to Molly. He'd lost her; he accepted that now. However, in the past thirty-eight hours, he'd gained three friends who he respected and would trust with his life.

And one of them had saved the life of his child.

# EPILOGUE

Luke sat on a velvet armchair in the Terracotta Room at Number 10, Downing Street. It was too early to drink, but as it was Christmas Day, he'd accepted the glass of port with his mince pie. At least he was no longer a suspect in the murder of Leander Amis.

Amelia, Jack, and Ruth sat on the long sofa facing a large fireplace without a fire. Ethan Cole, the prime minister, sat opposite him. No one else was in the room.

"Do you think it's over?" Cole asked. He looked at each of them in turn.

Luke shrugged. "At least the orange storm is subsiding."

"Yes," Cole said. "But unfortunately, we've lost half a county. The formation of what's now being called the East Cheshire Desert is a traumatic event for the country, and the government is committed to fully understanding what happened."

*Good luck with that*, Luke thought.

The transformation of east Cheshire was international news. Whole towns had been evacuated, and only just in time, as the sandstorm buried them beneath giant sand dunes.

"What will the government do?" Luke asked.

"We'll continue our search for the remains of the spacecraft." He paused for a sip of port. "But with that much sand, it's not an easy task."

There were reports of strange creatures wandering through the desert, although these had been denied by the government. A number of lush oases had also formed, but the flora and fauna bore little resemblance to anything on Earth.

"Have the sightings of alien wildlife been verified?" Luke asked.

"There are reports of strange sounds at night. And sightings of very odd creatures."

"The lizards?" Jack asked.

"No, other things."

The prime minister looked at Jack. "You should be awarded a medal for courage for what you did, but the rules of the Security Service are strict."

"I broke the rules. I accept responsibility for losing my job," Jack said.

"But still . . ." The prime minister paused to look at each of them. "What I'm about to say is confidential and can't be shared."

They nodded.

"I'm setting up a new intelligence service. Like MI5, it will include both researchers and an active intelligence unit. In fact, this is one of the reasons I invited you here. I wanted to ask all of you if you're interested in joining. The aims of the service will be to study the desert and everything inside it, and also to investigate any alien activity within our country."

"I thought the aliens were dead," Jack said.

"We hope so, but we can't yet be sure."

He smiled as he spoke, and Luke wondered how true this was.

"The acquisition of alien technology could hugely benefit our country. The alien humanoids proved themselves to be our enemy, but that's no reason not to study what they left behind. After all, this invasion could repeat itself."

*That, at least, was true,* Luke thought.

"The research centre will be within the outer wall that we're building around the desert." He smiled at Ruth. "We need a zoologist with expertise in alien lifeforms."

Luke noticed her eyes brighten.

"I'd love the chance to study alien lifeforms," she said. "But how independent will we be? And what will happen to any animals we find?"

"The unit will be independent, but of course, it will be a part of our national security network. And assuming the animals don't prove to be a threat to our nation, they'll be treated properly."

Ruth nodded. "I'd like to join."

"Excellent!" The prime minister looked at Jack. "Although we can no longer employ you within MI5, you'd be welcome in the new service. You'd be able to work closely with Ruth."

Luke held back a grin at the look that passed between Ruth and Jack.

"A sort of MI7?" Jack asked.

"In a way," the prime minister said.

Jack held Ruth's hand. "I'd be honoured to be a part of it."

The prime minister turned to Luke and Amelia. "You

both have special skills, and if you want, you're invited to join, too."

"Thank you, but I have a son to bring up," Luke said.

Amelia declined, too, without giving a reason.

"Well, if you change your mind..."

The meeting ended, and on the steps of 10 Downing Street, the four friends said goodbye.

"Do they know about the lobster?" Luke asked.

Ruth put a finger to her lips and grinned.

**FREE BOOKS**

If you're interested in learning more about me and receiving a free novelette and short story, visit nedmarcus.com and sign-up for my newsletter.

**PLEASE LEAVE A REVIEW**

If you enjoyed Orange Storm, please leave a review. Reviews can help a writer's work be read by more readers and help promote their career, so allowing more books to be written. Thank you!

## BOOKS BY NED MARCUS

### Blue Prometheus Series

- Young Aina #0
- Blue Prometheus #1
- The Darkling Odyssey #2
- Fire Rising #3

### Orange Storm Series

- Orange Storm #1
- The Orange Witch #2 (forthcoming)

## ABOUT THE AUTHOR

Ned Marcus is an author of fantasy and science fiction. He lives and writes in East Asia.

nedmarcus.com

# ACKNOWLEDGMENTS

Thank you to my editor, Parisa Zolfaghari; and to Owain McKimm, and other members of Taipei Fantasy and Sci-fi Writers' Group, for their help with this novel.

www.ingramcontent.com/pod-product-compliance
Lightning Source LLC
LaVergne TN
LVHW041905070526
838199LV00051BA/2496